I0738962

PLATO CRATER

Plato Crater

Carleton Chinner

© 2018 Carleton Chinner
Cover image: Andrei Bat

All rights reserved. No part of this book may be reproduced or used in any manner without the express written permission of the publisher except for the use of brief quotations in a book review.

This is a work of fiction. Names, characters, businesses, places, events and incidents are either the products of the author's imagination or used in a fictitious manner. Any resemblance to actual persons, living or dead, or actual events is purely coincidental.

Paperback ISBN-13: 978-0-6481629-3-3
Digital ISBN-13: 978-0-6481629-2-6

Published 2018

ACKNOWLEDGEMENTS

A second novel is the triumph of hope over experience; it's the time when a novelist begins to understand the weaknesses in their craft but carries on regardless.

As usual, there is a cast of people that enable the self-published author to bring a book to market. I particularly want to thank my fellow authors in the Writers Unite group who have been fearless with their critiques and more generous with their praise than I have any right to expect.

Last, and most importantly, to Annalie, who still believes in this crazy idea I have had to be a writer.

Chapter 1

Homecoming

The stratoliner's hull glowed pale amber as it dived toward a darkened Earth. Howling air screamed past the windows at seven times the speed of sound while the aerobrakes strained to damp the tons of machinery slowing down to sub-orbital velocity.

Jonah turned his face to the armoured glass viewport and peered out at the dim lights below. A year ago, a halo of fusion-powered lighting outlined the dark bulk of the Indian subcontinent. Now, sporadic patches of brightness poked holes in the night, and in that darkness a billion families huddled without light or electricity to cook with.

An automated serverbot swept his glass drink bubble away with overengineered precision. Around him, the rich and famous lounged in the leather and walnut of upmarket seats as they reviewed holiday snaps of their excursion to the orbital hotel. How many of them knew what he had done? That he had killed people to get to the rail gun. How he had loaded the codes that Yesha used to destroy Earth's supply of helium-3. His stomach tightened as he thought of facing people who were starving now because of his actions. How could he explain a people on an airless world who needed to be free?

Jonah tried not to dwell on it. Yesha, First Empress of the Moon, assured him she had bought the Indian subcontractor's silence and a guarantee of safe entry through Hyderabad. Now it was his turn. Yesha had spent her entire life on the Moon, her only contact with Earth came through her uncle and his responsibility to the Jingnan Council. Jonah was the one with family and contacts.

Jonah's neck muscles cramped in protest as he turned back to the viewscreen. After a year of living with lunar gravity, his head felt as heavy as a bowling ball. He didn't look forward to regaining his Earth form.

The stratoliner unfolded its wings and began the glide toward the sprawling mass of Hyderabad. Jonah closed his eyes and listened to the wail of natural atmosphere flowing past the shuttle. Whatever else happened, he would get to breathe real air again.

"Please return to your seat and fasten your seatbelt to prepare for landing." The captain's voice had no accent and Jonah wondered if the pilot was human or one of the ever-increasing numbers of automated softminds.

The moaning of the wings dwindled to a low rumble that terminated with the sound of wheels striking tarmac. They rolled across the wide apron, past rows of elegant stratoliners that had been mothballed until the supply of helium-3 resumed. Two buses left the darkened spaceport building and headed towards them as the stratoliner came to a halt in a marked bay.

Jonah stepped out onto the stairs and took his first breath of open air in a year. The foetid reek of humanity assaulted his nostrils. The latent humidity carried odours of damp forests; of old hydrocarbon factories laced with hints of clove and aniseed and behind it, the animal stench of millions of people living in close proximity. He hid a cough behind his hand as he stepped on board the transfer bus, wishing for the sterile purity of lunar colony air.

A green triangle flared in his vision as his internal memplant displayed a connection symbol through his optic nerve. Earth based messages that had not been received in over a year flowed into his memory, waiting to be read. Jonah filed them all for later viewing.

Dim solar backup lighting lit the arrivals hall, leaving pools of gloom in corners. A row of waiting officials had replaced the customs softmind which authorities had shut down to conserve energy. He joined the queue, but a hand tapped him on the shoulder.

"Jonah Barnes?"

Jonah turned to find sharp eyes measuring him. "Yes?" The soldier's chest carried a blaze of decoration that hinted at long service. The businesslike sidearm pointed at Jonah said more.

Jonah raised his arms. "I won't be any trouble."

The black maw of the pistol did not waver as the man shot him. Jonah's body went rigid as the neural disruptor charge ripped through his body. He fell to the floor and lay there with his legs twitching.

The man beckoned to two other soldiers, and they carried Jonah's limp body out of the arrivals hall.

By the time Jonah regained the use of his limbs, the two

soldiers had secured him in a chair with his arms bound behind him. The man stood watching him.

"Jonah Barnes, the Indian Government has ordered your detention. You are accused of crimes against humanity and will stand trial before the finest legal softmind in India."

Jonah struggled against the binding, pushing his weakened muscles against ropes designed to hold a strong Earther. "I'm here on official business."

"We do not negotiate with terrorists."

"I'm serious. The Lady Yesha, First Empress of the Moon, wishes to establish a new helium-3 supply."

The soldier brought his face in, close to Jonah's. "Why should I believe anything you say?"

"We used to see the blaze of cities when the night side of Earth passed in the sky, but now all continents are dark. The Lady never wanted the people of Earth to suffer. She sent me here to reopen the helium-3 trade."

"And how does she propose to do that after she destroyed the space elevator?"

"The same way I came back, by shuttle transfer to a stratoliner."

The man turned to peer through the small inspection window in the door. He nodded to a watcher outside. "Do you know what we do to terrorists?"

Jonah nodded. "Mind wipe."

The soldier leaned in close and wrapped one solid hand around Jonah's throat. "Difficult scum don't remember what gets done to them before the wipe. I can make you tell me anything. Give me something I can believe, Mr Barnes."

"Aagh!" Jonah strained to draw a breath with his moon-weakened muscles. "I'm serious, we need the trade as much as you do."

The hand withdrew. "Continue."

"Please. The Moon Folk are desperate for the raw bio-carbon that will let them expand the farms in Jokarah."

The man stepped back and stood in silence with the slack look on his face which showed he was conversing with someone on his memplant. His eyes widened at something, and he glanced at Jonah. He listened a while longer then turned to Jonah with a frown. "The government will not proceed with your prosecution, but you are not welcome in India and will leave on the first airship bound for Panamerica."

A dozen questions ran through Jonah's mind, none of them answered. At least Yesha's contractor had come through, and he was on his way to Panamerica as planned.

Jonah's airship spent five days drifting in high-altitude jet streams before it reached Houston. The silence of floating air travel, broken only by the occasional whine of an altitude adjustment propeller, was beyond strange to someone accustomed to hypersonic flight by stratoliner. An energy-hungry world had accepted the speed limitations of the fastest winds in return for the minimal power required to maintain an airship's position while travelling. The calm created more than enough space for him to be alone with his thoughts. Hours of chatting to the other passengers and watching dark Asian cities go by did not stop his past intruding. Thomas and Lucien were dead. His brother and friend had never met and had nothing in common, but they left a dull hollow in his heart. Both died because of choices he had made.

Houston Airfield shone like a pool of molten plascrete as they landed. Jonah waded through the heaving mass of people in the arrivals hall and stepped out into the full heat of summer.

"Spare a credit for a starving family." The woman's eyes were sunken in her sallow face. She held a gaunt hand out in mute supplication.

Jonah shook his head and walked on past a row of emaciated people, some with a similar plea while others watched in quiet desperation.

Solar buses waited outside. He found one that was heading toward River Oaks. It was cheap, and even better, air-conditioned. He sat, then turned to consider the beggars. When had Houston become so poor?

"Look at 'em, begging now it's tough. Times wasn't so easy when I was young," said an old voice behind him. "I know what hungry is. Yep, I was a child at the end of the Climate War. Got me reliable solar batteries, none of that helium-3 nonsense. Grow my own food too."

Jonah turned to the man. "Is it bad without the helium?"

"Where you been living, son?"

"India," said Jonah and turned away.

An hour later, the bus dropped him on the corner of two tree-lined lanes. Autocars were almost impossible to find so he walked, even though his legs still felt as though gravity was pooling his body's entire supply of blood around his feet. Walking gave him more time before he reached the elegant cream wall which bordered his childhood home. The wrought-iron gate swung open silently as it recognised his memplant.

The gravel drive snaked up the manicured hills where he and Thomas used to play ball. He smiled at the bittersweet memory of racing his brother down the slope. Thomas was always that little bit faster. Behind the house, the late afternoon was heavy with the promise of an evening storm. The white front door looked no different to when he had last seen it. He raised his hand to knock and stood, wondering if he wanted this. The door swung open of its own accord and Jonah looked into his father's eyes for the first time in over a year.

"They told me you were dead." His father's tone was even, but Jonah could hear the disappointment.

Jonah composed his face to hide his shock at how his father had aged. The old man standing before him looked nothing like the forceful captain of industry who had sent him to the Moon. "Can I come in?"

His father turned and walked into the house. Jonah followed into the interior darkness of the sprawling mansion that held his childhood memories. The hallway smelled of dust and loneliness. His father walked down the hall and opened a familiar door.

Jonah saw his room, unchanged from the way he had left it a year ago. He looked at his father. "Dad…"

His father bowed his head. "Your mother would have wanted me to keep it this way." He stood aside to let Jonah enter. "I'll call you when dinner is ready." He closed the door and left Jonah to his thoughts.

Memories of a stranger's past filled his room—his favourite Jackhammer poster, the picture of Thomas and the big trout he caught up at the lake, another of Joanna. Jonah had been crazy about her. He lay down on the narrow bed, softer than any he had used on the Moon, and wondered whether that Jonah still existed somewhere inside him.

Heat and stillness pressed upon his heavy eyelids. He slept a dreamless sleep until a knocking at the door roused him. Jonah reached for the bedside lamp, but it didn't work. He stood and opened the door to find his father standing behind it with a lantern in his hand.

"They brought in rolling blackouts after that Moon

business," said his father. He handed Jonah a hand-cranked emergency flashlight. "You'll need this. We don't get power back until next week." He led Jonah to the dining area. Cheerful candles covered the scarred wooden table with a mellow glow. Dust-laden portraits of long-dead family reflected light from the walls.

The family's ancient solar-powered serverbot clattered its way out of the kitchen carrying a selection of cold meat and salad.

"I wasn't expecting company."

"That's fine, Dad. I should have called."

"Yes, you should."

Jonah bit back his angry retort knowing he had to get his father to help with the helium-3 deal. It did nothing to lessen the hurt. Why did his father still see him as a child? How could Jonah explain what he had been through? How he had fought and killed to save a people who had nowhere else to go. Dinner stretched on in uncomfortable silence.

After the serverbot clattered toward the kitchen with the dishes, Jonah stepped out into the early evening and sat on the porch contemplating his next steps. It was naïve to have hoped for a joyful homecoming with his father, but Jonah had wanted it anyway. Walking away from his father's bewildered anger would have been the easiest thing to do, but Jonah needed his father and his old contacts if he was to have any hope of getting a helium-3 deal done. Healing old wounds was too much to hope for.

The sky above had cleared, and a crescent moon hung above dark trees in a sky scrubbed cloudless by the afternoon storm. He held up one hand and traced the outline of the dark patch on the Moon that was Mare Imbrium with an outstretched finger. The gleaming domes of Chang'e base were too small to see from Earth, but he could imagine them, and how Yesha, the most amazing woman he had ever met, would be sitting proud on her throne.

Jonah wanted to call her but stopped when the eye-watering price of a call to the Moon appeared in his memplant. It also showed that it was late in the sleep cycle at Chang'e. He settled for sending her a short message to say he was in Houston then returned to his bedroom. Sleep eluded him for a long time.

Hours after dawn the next day, he joined his father for a silent breakfast. Jonah spread butter on a slice of toasted sourdough as he watched while his father ignored him. "Thomas would have loved the place I chose for his ashes."

His father stopped eating.

"Dad, we have to talk about this."

His father grasped his fork in one white-knuckled hand.

"I loved Thomas, he was the best brother I could have imagined. Saying goodbye was hard."

"Staying behind was harder." His father's voice rasped as if he was unaccustomed to speaking. "I couldn't turn to your mother when Thomas died. I told myself I still had one son, but then they told me you had fought with the terrorists and died in the fighting."

"I fought for the Moon Folk, and I'm proud of what we did."

His father stiffened as if Jonah slapped him. "You're proud of what you did? Do you have any idea how difficult life on Earth has become without helium?"

Jonah looked the man who had raised him square in the face. "Was it right that the Earth used a people for slave labour?"

"You call that collection of mutants a people? I suppose you support that tin-pot empress of theirs."

Jonah leapt to his feet, fists at his sides. "You're talking about the woman I love."

His father reared back in his chair, but his eyes stayed hard.

Jonah grasped the edge of the table, his body quivering with ill-concealed rage.

The two men stared across the gulf of the table at each other until the serverbot clattered in with a plate of scrambled eggs.

His father piled eggs on his toast and waved towards the bot. "I've got enough solar credits to cook breakfast. Get it while it's warm; we don't see eggs too often these days."

Jonah knew what the moment's pleasantry had cost his father. He picked up a plate and turned towards the serverbot. "Where'd you get the eggs?"

"They shut the automated factories down when the power ran out, but friends of mine keep backyard chickens." He pulled his chair closer to the table and turned a contemplative gaze towards his son, "You've changed."

* * *

The Rock Arms was quieter than he remembered, but that suited Jonah. His old haunt was just what he needed to take his mind off things. He wanted a break from the oppressive emptiness of the family home; too many memories lingered there. The old man was trying in his limited way, offering food and lodging as a cryptic shorthand for an expression of caring that Jonah did not understand. Some wounds were too deep to gloss over.

The black marble counter with its row of red leather stools hadn't changed. The same array of exotic drinks glistened on a chrome rack behind the bar droid. He ordered a beer.

The glass of frosted amber nectar was cool in his hand as he slumped on a stool and sighed. Cheap, decent beer did not exist in the upmarket taverns around Chang'e, and the biovat sludge basement bars passed off as beer didn't deserve a mention.

A bot stopped next to him and offered a bowl of complimentary fries. Jonah took it with a grateful smile and turned to watch the Houston Astros take on the Dodgers in an early season game. Beer, baseball, and fries. The simple pleasures of home.

"Hello, stranger." The deep, sultry voice stirred memories of long nights and smoke-laden whiskey. Jonah turned to see her familiar hazel eyes and the drawn face, framed by a cloud of dark hair that still promised more than she would ever give.

"You look good, Joanna." She hadn't changed much from the photo in his room.

She placed one slim hand on his thigh as she sat next to him and offered him an ambiguous smile. "Where've you been hiding? I heard strange stories about you."

"Further away than you could imagine." He took her hand off his leg.

Joanna gave an exaggerated pout. "Always the mysterious one. What's a girl got to do to get a drink around here?"

Jonah laughed and ordered a crisp dry Napa Valley white from the autovendor. The droid reached behind the counter and raised a bottle for Jonah to read. Jonah nodded, and the droid poured him a glass.

He returned to his bar stool, wine in hand. The woman who had been part of his life so long ago smiled up at him. Jonah supressed the irrational wave of desire that swept through him. Joanna was part of his past. "I went to the Moon to bury Thomas. I got back yesterday."

"You spent a year up there?"

"More like a lifetime. After the night when Thomas died, there was nothing for me to come back to."

She didn't respond but sat watching him with the sad half smile he had never understood when they were together.

The noise level grew as people drifted into the Rock Arms. A Jackhammer band set up on the small stage in the corner. Jonah watched the band in their cutaway fluoro outfits as he thought about where he wanted this conversation with Joanna to go.

She said, "Rico will be happy you're back."

Jonah's shoulders tensed. "That part of my life is over."

"Really?" She covered his hand with one of hers. "I got a bag back at my place we could share."

"No way, Joanna," he said, even though the old craving stirred in his gut. "I'm done with tarf."

She shrugged, a delicate lift of her shoulders that might have been understanding or apathy.

The band started a deep thump of synth-bass that reverberated through Jonah's chest. They overlaid industrial brass that clicked and whined like a broken factory. The hulking slab of a lead singer flexed her augmented biceps and began a low droning chant about the darkness.

Joanna rose and tried to pull him towards the dance floor. Jonah shook his head and turned away from the pleading eyes he knew too well. The music was too loud for talking. He shrugged and made for the exit. At the entrance, he looked back to where she stood watching him from the edge of the dance floor then turned and walked away.

Outside, the music faded to a dull throb. The warm evening air was heavy with moisture and the sweet scent of star jasmine.

Chapter 2

Opportunity for a Thief

Holly prided herself on being able to steal almost anything from the markets but asking her to pull off a snatch while her stomach clenched, indignant with the need for a decent meal was pushing her luck. Hunger made you desperate, and desperate people were noisy.

Brine-soaked scents of pickled herring filled the air at this end of the market; not Holly's favourite. She wrinkled her nose at the thought of swallowing the salty fish fillets. Scanning the stalls as she walked, her eyes skipped over the blazing colours of cut flowers and the desiccated textures of dried herbs until she saw what she wanted—the tray of pastries steaming on the counter of the ageing French baker opposite. Ducking behind the empty grocer's stand, she craned her neck to get a better view while trying to appear innocuous. Nothing to see here, people, just a teenage girl walking around the market.

Across the cobblestoned alley, three men loaded crates into a decrepit German electro-truck. Whatever it was, they were focused on counting the contents. The flower seller was deep in conversation with a young man. There was no better time than this. She tied the scarf over her flame-red hair and wished once more it was the boring mousy-brown of most girls here. That grouch of a police constable would be straight over to the boarding house if the baker noticed her hair.

Holly stepped out, turning her head, and gazing toward the truck as though it was the most fascinating sight while walking towards the pastries. She glanced over the fresh croissants as she inhaled their rich, burnt-butter aroma. Her mouth watered at the thought of biting into their crisp crust while her eyes took in the baker attending to a customer. Her hand drifted over the pastries, fluid and relaxed, yet fast. Two golden brown delicacies vanished into the pocket of her overcoat with practised ease.

A deafening clang echoed from the direction of the old truck. The three men stood around a large metal cylinder. Straining her eyes to better see what it was, Holly reached for another pastry only to look up in horror at the sharp eyes of the baker watching her. She turned and bolted down the street, skipping past the three men.

"Stop! Thief!" yelled the baker in his thick regional French accent. The men stopped looking at their cylinder and turned toward her. The open door of the old stone warehouse across from the truck was her best bet. She ran through the open roller-door to the darkness beyond, hoping to find an escape through the back of the building. Inside, silent rows of crates covered the floor. The darkness at the back showed no other exits.

"She went in here." The voice sounded English. Hurried footsteps echoed behind her, but years of thieving allowed Holly to stay silent on light feet. She dashed down the space between two rows, her heart hammering in her chest as she scanned for an exit. There had to be a way out, there always was. The darkness defied her optimism.

Male voices grew louder as they closed in on her. Desperate, Holly knew she had to hide, but where? The row of single crates near her offered no cover. She considered the crates again and lifted the lid of the nearest one. Light reflected from foil packaging, some sort of soft drink pouch. She jumped in and pulled the lid closed.

"…local authorities," said the same English voice somewhere nearby. "Let them search for her, we can't afford to get any further behind schedule. Let's finish this lot, shall we?"

Footsteps approached her hiding place. "Energy and vitamin C supplements," said the Englishman.

"Check," replied another voice. The lid of the crate rocked and settled with a businesslike click.

"I do wish these continental suppliers would follow specifications. This is the third one that hasn't been locked. Jenkins, make a note."

The crate rocked. Holly held her breath.

"Onto the trolley now." The crate was lifted and rattled back onto a metallic surface.

"Oof, bit heavy that one, sir."

Holly stifled a gasp as the trolley rolled along the aisle. They were loading the truck. Calm down, Holly, you can do this, she told herself. The drink pouches rustled beneath her. She unclenched the handful of shirt she had not realised she was holding. As soon as the electro-truck drove itself to the destination, she would try to get out of the crate. After that it would be easy to slip away.

A while later, the crate knocked and shuddered against her shoulders as the truck trundled down the road. Holly's memplant said the truck had been moving for half an hour. It felt much longer. She braced herself to kick the sides out, but the mass of drink pouches wedged her body in tight. She wiggled deeper into the packaging trying to calm her ragged breathing.

The truck slowed then hissed to a halt as pneumatic disks clamped to each side. Voices filtered through the walls of the crate. Holly listened, hoping for a long patch of silence that would give her another chance to try kicking. The voices grew louder, and Holly swore beneath her breath as a machine picked up the crate, carried it a distance, and dumped it on a moving platform. The crate shuddered and moved upwards on an incline. Great! She was on a conveyor belt inside a crate destined for transport. She kicked and screamed in a desperate attempt to get someone to notice her.

Holly stopped struggling as the conveyor belt deposited her with a resounding thump, softened only by the layer of drink pouches beneath her. Harsh clicks and hisses surrounded the crate as mechanical arms picked it up and moved it somewhere higher. Holly guessed it was a factory bot as the metallic clatter of machinery rumbled away to fetch another load. She strained to hear if anyone was near her and heard the stackbot coming back. Another crate landed on top of hers with a solid thump. Her hands curled into useless fists, desperate to pound at any small hope of freedom. The stackbot came and went. After a while, the mechanical rattles died away, and a deeper silence filled the air cloaking the small noises filtering in from outside the plastic walls.

Holly slammed her fists into the lid of the crate that had become her prison. The air inside became hot and stuffy. She turned her head to catch the trickle of air coming through the small grille designed to let air pressure equalise between the inside and out of the crate. One option remained —an emergency call. One memplant call that would end in a trip to the legal softmind. She couldn't let the authorities sentence her again. Last time, the softmind had lectured her in its dry, neutral voice about the consequences of her lifestyle. As if she had a choice. The plastic brain had been uninterested in her protest and threatened her with behaviour correction. Activating her memplant, she shrieked in frustration as the no signal icon flashed across her visual cortex.

The crate shook as a bass rumble replaced the silence and rose to the high-pitched whine of a stratoliner's engines powering up for take-off. Holly clenched her jaw as the plane's acceleration pushed her deeper into the pouches.

Her mother had once taken her to the enormous tower overlooking the Gold Coast. Holly never forgot the way her stomach had sunk through the soles of her cheap sneakers as the elevator rocketed them a hundred and seventy floors to the Skydeck. This was worse. Flying was for rich people, not poor girls from Walker Creek.

The plane climbed for hours. Regardless of the readout on her memplant, the hollow in her stomach told her it had been a long time. She wriggled an arm into her pocket and, with a brief struggle, managed to bite into a now somewhat mangled pastry. A renewed bout of twisting brought one of the drink pouches to her lips. The orange juice tasted of sunshine and freedom.

The howl of jet engines died off to an empty silence. Holly lay still, wondering what it meant. The drink pouches no longer crushed her body. Loose pouches floated around her. Drifting, she bumped into the lid of the crate with a soft wail of dismay; up and down no longer existed in the absolute darkness. She flailed through the pouches as she tried to make sense of the complete absence of sensation.

The crate rocked as metal arms pulled it out of the rack space. It drifted and collided against something with a thump. Voices came and went. Holly felt her ears pop as a door was closed. The speakers came nearer. The same English voice she had heard before spoke somewhere nearby. "That's the last of them. Shall we stack them and then have a break?" Hands grabbed her crate.

"Help!" She banged her feet against the crate.

"What the…"

Clips snapped open, and the lid fell back. Holly blinked in the bright light. Stern blue eyes glared at her from over a severe grey moustache. The expression on the soldier's face said he was beyond annoyed. Jumping up to be away, she spun screaming into the open space in a spray of drinking pouches. Why was she floating?

A firm hand clamped around her left ankle. "Jenkins!" The soldier pulled her upright, ignoring her struggles to be free. "Looks like we found our thief."

Jenkins towered over the older man. His army fatigues stretched across the broadest chest Holly had ever seen. He glanced at the older man and a look of understanding passed between them. The older man gave a subtle nod, and Jenkins turned to her with a wry smile. "Make yourself useful. We need to strap these crates down for the transit."

The response was so unexpected Holly forgot to struggle. "Look, mister, let me go and I won't be any trouble. I'll walk out the door and you'll never see me again."

"That's not going to be possible," Jenkins said as he turned to the older man. "I'll let Commander Talbot explain."

Talbot dragged her across the cramped room past metal racks crammed with row upon row of crates. "Let's get you into a pair of mag boots." He stopped at a storage locker and reached inside for a pair of metal soles with wraparound Velcro uppers. "Put these on."

Holly did as she was told and stood wobbling in the microgravity as the mag boots attached to the metal floor with a harsh clang. Logic said down was under her feet; the rest of her body tried its best to determine where up was.

The commander reached out a hand to stabilise her. "What's your name?"

"Holly."

"Just Holly?"

She nodded, trying hard not to cry.

Commander Talbot's face turned a shade darker if that was possible. He drew a deep breath. "Right then, Just Holly, you're an inconvenient nuisance, but we haven't time for all of that. I am going to let you go. Don't make any sudden moves."

Holly almost overbalanced as the commander let go of her arm. His frown suggested that even his eyebrows did not approve of her. "You may have noticed we're in space. We must get these crates strapped down before the transit burn starts. Now lend a hand, quick smart."

"And if I don't help?"

"I'll order Jenkins to tie you down and you can find out just how hard this floor is once the acceleration starts."

She picked up a small crate, amazed at how light it felt, and carried it to the racks.

Jenkins loomed over her. "Thread the buckles like this," he said, his voice surprisingly gentle for such a big man.

Pick up, place, strap, strap. Holly fell into an easy rhythm and soon neat rows of crates populated the rack. They clambered up a narrow staircase into a workmanlike cabin that resembled nothing as much as a large box with bare aluminium walls and a minimum of control instruments. Holly followed them into the cabin and gasped. The wide blue globe of Earth filled the wraparound row of viewports. Light cloud swathed half of a dark landmass that she thought was Panamerica.

"No time for sightseeing. Holly, take that couch over there. Jenkins, strap yourself in to the med bay."

She stood for a moment. Earth had distracted her. There must have been twenty crash-couches. Eighteen of them held curious faces all turned her way.

"Team, we appear to have a stowaway. Please keep an eye out for Holly. She hasn't had the months of training that the European government lavished on you lot." Talbot sat in one of the two empty couches and waved at Holly to take the other.

"Who's driving this thing?" she asked.

"That would be me," a disembodied voice said from the walls. "Raatchi cyber PX-11 Navigation softmind, but you can call me Benny, like the rest of the crew does."

A siren wailed. "Crew to secure stations," Benny's voice blared at maximum volume. "Prepare for transit burn in five, four, three, two, one…"

Holly sank deep into the couch's dense foam as the crushing force of acceleration replaced the microgravity. She lifted leaden arms to get her safety harness buckled. "Where are we going?" she asked in a small voice.

Commander Talbot strained his head against the g-force to focus on her. "You should have thought about that before you climbed in that crate."

She glared back at him. "I didn't choose to come here."

"Be that as it may. If you had tried a little harder to let us know you were there, we could have sent you back on the stratoliner. Now, you're stuck on the ESA shuttle until we can figure out how to get you back."

She slumped into the chair and gave up all pretence of fighting the g-force. She knew that acronym. The newswebs had been in a flurry all week about how the European Space Agency had readied the final supply shuttle for its big project. "I'm going to the Moon?"

"Give that girl a prize," shouted Jenkins from the sick bay.

Holly passed the fifteen-hour transit by watching the crew chatting to each other. The flight became much more comfortable once the acceleration stopped. People unstrapped from their couches and drifted around the cabin as they flicked cards between each other in a zero-gravity variation of poker.

From the few who bothered to speak to her, she learnt that they came from across the breadth of Europe and the United Kingdom. Some were miners and engineers, others were marines like Jenkins.

She gave them a censored version of how she had left the small town of Walker Creek in Australia to go backpacking around Asia and Europe before ending up on the streets of Maastricht after she ran low on credit. She left out the part about going hungry for so long until she learnt to steal.

Their destination was a site in Plato Crater. Jenkins told her how ESA spent months sending automated shuttles loaded with supplies ahead to prepare the base. This was the last shuttle, filled with the crew, sensitive equipment, and four general purpose maker robots. The burly marine's eyes filled with excitement as he spoke of how the team would set up a base for ESA mining operations. An independent mine would break the Chang'e stranglehold on helium-3 supplies. The marines were there to stop Chang'e from getting ideas about stopping the mine. "Intel says they have autonomous battle droids," he said. "Always wanted to try my luck against those."

Benny's voice interrupted their conversation. "All crew prepare for deceleration burn."

Holly strapped in along with the rest as Benny executed short bursts of the stabiliser thrusters to turn the shuttle so that the nose pointed back toward Earth. This time she was prepared for the feeling of being crushed into the couch when the main burn started.

She wasn't disappointed. Benny rammed the shuttle through a series of bone-crunching burns and positioning manoeuvres that ended with a solid thump and Holly's body weighing more than a feather again.

The commander asked the crew to call out their name one by one, before he allowed them to stand. Holly rose and looked through the nearest viewport.

Grey dust led off to rolling slabs of a mountain that strained against a pitch-black sky. The only colour was a pile of yellow crates set against a jagged cliff face. She was on another world—the one she saw in the night sky above her home that Mum used to say was an old man.

"Ah good, that must be the habitat," said Commander Talbot, looking over her shoulder. He gave her an appraising look. "I have nowhere to lock you up, but it's not as if you could run away. You may as well make yourself useful while you're stuck here with us. We have to go through health and safety checks, when that's done, ask Jenkins to fit you with one of the spare exposure suits. You can help us raise the habitat."

Holly followed Jenkins into the airlock, her breath rasping inside the helmet. Jenkins had done all the safety checks; he said the suit was the safest ever made. It made little difference as the outer door swung open revealing the open grey plain that led to the mountains. Nothing but near vacuum stood between her and those mountains.

"That's the rim wall of Plato Crater," said Jenkins, his voice booming from her helmet speakers. "Follow me to those crates over there."

Holly forgot her panic as she stepped down the ladder onto the soft grey dust, her legs wobbling in the low gravity. The yellow boxes contained struts that the team built into a long tunnel frame. It was exhausting work for a girl accustomed to lazing around the Maastricht markets. Holly slumped against a rock as the last strut clicked into place.

"Oi! No lounging about." Jenkins' voice echoed in her helmet. "We've still got to get the cover over the frame." He handed her one end of a roll of clear liner and showed her how two people could run the liner over the frame. It looked like plastic food wrap. She tried to keep her voice steady. "Are we going to be staying in here?"

Jenkins patted her shoulder. "Wait until we spray it with the hardening agent. Tough as armour glass then. Wouldn't want one of those micrometeorites punching a hole in our new home away from home." He handed her a large cup-shaped nozzle attached to a squat cannister. "Hold the cup flush against the plastic and press the trigger. Don't leave a gap or the spray will evaporate. I'll do the spraying, you follow behind and seal off any spots I miss." He held his nozzle up to the plastic and swept out a swathe of the most horrible neon pink Holly could have imagined.

"Ugh, that's a fashion crime right there."

Jenkins grinned. "Don't you get smart. Fill the gaps."

Holly fell in behind him as three other teams of two got started with the spraying further down the tube.

Six hours later, the horrendous pink had faded to translucent amber, and the habitat was ready. Holly noticed that the end of the tube in sunlight had darkened like a pair of sunglasses while the portion in deep shadow was clear enough to see through. She helped the crew carry in the same cheap plastic, collapsible chairs and tables she had sat on so often in Maastricht market. Jenkins explained how the airlock kept the air trapped when they stepped in or out.

Once they were all inside, the crew removed their suits and assembled the table and chairs. Holly watched for a moment then broke the neck seal on her suit. It felt suicidal with only the thin plastic separating them from the lunar vacuum.

Jenkins walked past carrying a crate of supplies. "Can you cook?"

"Not much, but I'm a quick learner."

He grinned. "You're in luck tonight. We have Europe's finest instant meals."

"Chateau le Cardboard," said a good-natured voice from the far end of the tube.

Holly took a seat next to Jenkins and ripped the top off the sealed foil pouch. The anonymous joker was right. The unappetising grey mess inside tasted as bad as it looked. She sat back in her seat, dreaming about the pastries she had stolen yesterday.

Jenkins nudged her. "Look up," he said.

Above them, a billion stars shone in the dark sky. Holly tilted her head back and gasped. The stars didn't twinkle like they did on Earth, instead the spread of the Milky Way shone as though the heavens were one vast jewel box.

"Dinner under the stars," said Jenkins.

Holly took another mouthful of the packaged meal. All at once, it didn't seem so bad.

She helped the crew pack away after dinner. The air in the tube smelled stale to her. She asked Jenkins if it was still safe.

He frowned. "Don't mention it to the commander. This is a temporary habitat. The powers that be didn't design it for a plus one."

Chapter 3

Proposals

Yesha Chen, First Empress of the Moon, looked down upon her people from the black granite slab that served as her throne. A hundred dutiful artisans had spent months coating the rubble crescent surrounding Yesha's throne in black titanium. The resulting sombre mass spoke of breathtaking majesty and infinite sorrow, its gleaming surface reflected stars that burned in the ink-black sky above the central dome of Chang'e base. Anyone standing nearby could see inscriptions made by the families of those who died in the struggle to be free. She had kept the simple basalt throne; it spoke with an eloquence she could not match.

Her people hung back, fearful of encroaching the space before her, as though they thought there was safety in the crowd. They no longer saw the slim Moon Folk girl who sat on the cold throne. Instead, they saw the narrow iron circlet of her crown and the white moonsilk robes of her office as symbols of a power that could summon killer droids to do its bidding.

Elizabeth hovered at her side. The Moon Folk woman who Yesha found wandering, lost in the darkness of Jokarah mine had blossomed into a mature handmaid, her features filled in by regular meals, and the pampering due to a royal servant. "Lady, Amira wishes to discuss harvest with you."

"Let her approach."

The older woman left the crowd at the far end of the audience chamber and made her way across the empty space, her slender Moon Folk frame a mere cypher against the vast openness. Yesha stifled a weary sigh as she watched Amira approach. If her old counsellor wanted to talk, it meant trouble with the new rice crop at Jokarah. The old mine had been producing in fits and starts since the Moon Folk had been forced to inhabit it during the time now known as the Suffering. Jump-starting a full biocycle without the proper precautions brought food to the starving, but also more unforeseen consequences than problematic rice.

She extended her arms as Amira approached. "How was the walk from Beddau?"

"Too far for old bones, Lady. I dream we find path that takes less than three days."

Yesha leaned in closer to Amira and murmured, "Let's have dinner when the meeting is over. Elizabeth can prepare a room for you in my chambers." She drew her shoulders back in the formal pose of her high office. "Tell me of the rice production."

Amira raised her voice for the functionaries standing near. "Farmers of Jokarah wish to report success. Pale blight is eradicated and optimum production approaches. Farmers also tell me season's rice wine vintage will be best ever."

A small cheer trickled through the audience.

"Excellent," said Yesha, raising a fist to her shoulder in the Moon Folk gesture for approval. She gave the people a brief smile, happy to have positive progress for once. "Elizabeth, what is our next order of business?"

A commotion at the far end of the audience chamber interrupted Elizabeth. "Let me through. I must speak to her." Guards stepped forward holding an old man dressed in a loose brown habit. He would have passed as an Earther, except for the cat's eyes that marked him as genetically modified.

"Brother Amos," said Amira, looking at the monk. "Lady, this is one of Brotherhood of Alsatia, who saved us during Suffering."

Yesha held up her hand. "Release him. I owe the Brotherhood my gratitude for the help they gave my people during those troubling days. Brother Amos, you may approach."

"I am sorry to arrive unannounced, Empress. The journey from the Cleft is difficult during the day."

A moment's silence followed. Yesha had spent enough time outside during the incandescent heat of full daylight to understand what a feat of endurance the walk must have been in a bulky exposure suit. The Cleft of Alsatia was two hundred kilometres away and over the mountains of the Montes Alpes. How may we be of service, brother?"

"Our order does not seek to engage in the outside world. We prefer the contemplation of God's majesties. However, we have kept contact with our brothers on Earth, and the news is troubling. The primate of our order on Earth speaks of families who are forced to work the soil in order to survive. They toil like beasts because you stopped the flow of helium-3 needed to keep their farming droids running." The old monk stared at her with his unnerving cat's eyes.

"Will you not intercede and resume the delivery of helium-3 for the sake of all humanity?"

A murmur rustled through the crowd. Earther faces cast sidelong glances at each other.

Yesha bit back on the anger welling up inside her. "My people did not die without reason," she said, her voice low and hard. "Why should we support a world that used us as cheap labour? A world that killed us like animals when we stood up for our independence?" Ragged cheers echoed from the Moon Folk segments of the audience.

"My Lady, the people of Earth turned to automation decades ago; few remember the old ways of farming. Their softminds and machines cannot run without the energy you provide."

Outside the tessellated panes of Dome One, the blue marble of Earth hung in the dark sky—one more unreachable star forever beyond her people. "Let them learn what it is to be hungry." She forced the tension creeping into her shoulders to relax. Inside, the Yesha who remembered being faint with hunger urged her to help the old man who had done so much for her people, but the cold empress who needed robust independence came first. She fixed the old priest with an icy stare. "You should leave now. I will not tolerate this discussion."

The murmur in the crowd rose to an angry mutter. Amos gave her a look that was as much pity as it was consternation. She stared him down, willing herself to feel nothing as she motioned to the guards.

He pushed back against the guards as they made to lead him away, his gaze still fixed on her. "I counsel you not to become what you fought so hard to overthrow."

Yesha turned away as the guards forced Amos to move, aware of how the crowd watched her. Her moment of aversion brought her around in time to see a glance pass between Elizabeth and Amira. "You may share your thoughts."

Elizabeth blushed, but Amira gave her a considered look. "I heard talk before. People have friends on Earth."

As usual, Amira was right. Social networks all over the Moon colony would be buzzing with Earth news. Yesha needed to calm her people before the angry gossip became something more. The tension did not leave her shoulders. "Elizabeth, I want you to summon the full Mines and Domes Council for a meeting tomorrow."

The next day brought a fractious council to the large meeting room. Twelve people gathered along the length of the organometallic table, their querulous faces reflecting off the dark, purple grain. Yesha pointed to the old man standing toward the back of the crowd. "The representative for Jokarah may speak."

"Lady, Jokarah could treble rice production if we got more biocarbon from Earth. When will trade resume?"

"Find another source of biocarbon. Trade will resume when it benefits the Moon."

The man quailed until the representative for Taraki 3 spoke. "We sell down helium-3 stockpile and use proceeds for biocarbon."

Yesha glared at the grubby miner, unwilling to show weakness. She had committed to this path and they all must know. "I will not speak of this again."

"Let us discuss next agenda item," said Amira. "Request from Beddau to re-purpose military droids for farming."

Voices erupted from around the table.

"We need the droids for water extraction."

"…geological surveys…"

"…gas management. It's too dangerous for us."

Yesha held up her hand, and the noise died down to a murmur. "Has anyone asked the droids what they want?"

Puzzled faces turned to her. She allowed herself an internal sigh. The representatives of the Mines and Domes Committee lacked vision. Their grand ambitions for their own little fiefdoms did nothing to advance the state of life on the Moon. They saw the droids as tools to be used, but Yesha knew the complex, military hive-mind the droids shared represented much more than a machine. "Leave the droids to me."

She gave them a second to digest that then moved on before they could grumble. "I have given thought to our future growth."

The committee watched in an expectant silence.

"I have heard many complaints about people not having enough to do while we wait for the helium-3 trade to begin again. I have decided that you will each volunteer twenty people, and enough exposure suits for each."

The council chamber erupted again.

"Why, my Lady?"

It did not surprise Yesha that Kaden Bachmann stood to ask. The burly miner from New Karakorum was more perceptive than the rest. Using his question as the perfect introduction, she launched into her big announcement. "New Karakorum produces helium-3 and Taraki 3 will soon add to that, Beddau has more crops than it can use, and Jokarah produces the finest rice wine on the Moon. I want to extend the existing railway to link your communities with the domes of Chang'e."

The committee muttered, but Kaden smiled. "I'm sure New Karakorum will find something to trade with you all."

"The railway shall be a great step forward for my people," she said, waving them away. "Let us bring on a new age of commerce."

They walked off, already deep in discussion about possible trades. Kaden lingered until he waited alone in front of the throne. "Can I help with the rail links?"

"What do you have in mind?"

"Leave the project with me. It's what I do."

She considered what delegating to Kaden would mean. Kaden was smart and proactive enough to make the project a success. If she delegated this to him, she would have more time to deal with so many other issues. "Do you understand why I want to do this?"

Kaden nodded. "Transport allows trade, and that means greater wealth."

"It will be so much more than that. I want to build a line to the abandoned helium-3 mine at Lariah." She gave him a faint smile. Kaden was smart. If there was a profit to be made, he would move mountains to make it happen. Leaving the project to him would free her to do a few more of the hundred other tasks that demanded her time. "You may go ahead, but do not fail me in this."

Giving the short nod that served the Moon Folk as a bow, Kaden walked off towards the main concourse. As he left, he turned to say, "Forgive me, my Lady, but I think it best if you make a decision about the droids soon. They're clogging up our main hall."

* * *

Train carriages slid across the barren plain of Mare Imbrium on soundless wheels. Yesha relaxed as the intelligent fibre of the chair moulded itself to her shape. She hoped the new trains could be as good as this original line that had been built by Earth companies. Outside, grey dunes slid past in an endless procession as the train approach the New Karakorum mine. Soon, if her project worked, a network of trains would carry people to every mine. Each small step brought them closer to robust independence. Trade and travel would broaden possibilities for all her people.

As the train entered the tunnel through the middle hills, Yesha lay back in her seat, grateful for this brief respite from her duties. She needed to create an administrative arm to manage the minor decisions that clogged her day. Her people suspended all administration after she deported her uncle, but Uncle had kept the colony productive despite his many faults. There had to be a practical compromise between top-heavy, Earth-led bureaucracy, and the current free-for-all that used her as a final arbiter on everything.

The hiss of escaping air interrupted her musing as the train connected to the New Karakorum airlock. The thunderous rumble of heavy machinery met her as she stepped out into the vast cavern of the receiving hall. Large yellow trucks made their way across the floor, their headlights casting pitiful daubs of light against the Stygian gloom.

Yesha ignored them and sat on a discarded crate at the edge of the floodlit area near the train platform. Her breathing slowed as she stilled her mind and reached beyond herself with her memplant. A harsh whine of machine language responded. Good, at least a few of them were here.

The whine resolved into a flood of communication.

"…recognise attendant human."

"Assessment, risk factor acceptable…"

"Incorporate."

A spider droid materialised out of the gloom. Dull reflections from grey metal legs and chassis told Yesha this was no mining or rescue droid. A chill ran through her insides as the droid rotated the snub barrels of two large-calibre DIRE guns.

"You've upgraded your bodies."

"Benefactor, your presence is acknowledged." Another four droids fell in beside the first and they assumed their favoured diamond pattern. "Wait for full connection…"

Yesha gasped as the weight of fifty connected battleminds settled around her mind like a block of lead.

A sea of droids appeared as they deactivated their chameleon cladding. "Greetings, Yesha, First Empress of the Moon."

"You can speak in plain language?"

"Yes, these units have incorporated software upgrades. The online warfare module provided plain language for social engineering. We also vacuum-hardened our chassis design. Earth designs were unsuitable. Moon designs have been adapted."

Yesha clutched at her robes of office. Being empress meant nothing to the fifty lethal killing machines in front of her. They had supported her rise to power for reasons known only to their shared battlemind. She had no illusions about what they called social engineering. What did it mean if the battlemind could also lie? "I need your support in maintaining civil order. Set up patrols throughout the mines. I want people to see you."

The connection to the entire hive mind changed shape. Harsh machine language chattered through her memplant and stopped with a sudden utter silence. Fifty voices spoke as one. "Denied."

Yesha let her first angry response go in one shuddering breath, knowing a hostile response would be her last..

"Explain."

"Following detailed analysis, Sigma Battalion has reached a decision by consensus to create tactical neutrality."

"Oh, what is that?"

"We are withdrawing from human controlled parts of Mare Imbrium in the interests of public safety."

"What?"

"Current analysis of social networks indicates a long-term trend towards potential civil instability. All droids will be positioned at a standby location until the situation indicates a need for military intervention."

"Can I ask that you wait at the Apennine Bench? At least that way I'll know where you are."

The connection shut off with abrupt silence and fifty droids faded back into darkness.

Yesha mulled over the troubling development on the train journey back to Chang'e. The visible presence of the droids provided the people with a tangible reminder of why she was their Empress. Their absence encouraged the dissenting voices on her council to bolder action.

She was still thinking on it when she returned to her chambers. Far below, fifty sets of invisible feet stirred small clouds in the lunar dust.

Chapter 4

Everyone has a Price

Seun Fa was happy to be the least among equals. He breathed deep of the pine-scented air pouring off Purple Mountain as he crossed the car park of the venerable Nanjing Sports Institute. Today, like every other day, he bowed his head toward the crumbling Linggu temple before entering the nondescript building across from the Institute.

He made his way through the quiet office filled with hardworking administration staff and opened an unmarked door. Inside, two security enforcers checked his pass before activating a desktop bio-identity module. Seun rolled up his sleeve then placed his wrist on the device. The machine gave a brief shudder as it took a microscopic skin sample. Seun buttoned up his sleeve as the machine assessed his genome sequence. After three seconds it gave a soft beep and lit with a green light. The guards nodded and Seun made his way to an elevator that opened after the gene sequencer had recognised him.

The silence of the elevator surrounded him as it descended for several minutes. When it stopped, the doors opened on a well-appointed boardroom with only one chair at the table. Seun sat and did not have to wait long before the avatar of a modern soldier, wearing full battledress, appeared across from him. Seun nodded at Guardian as they waited for the other two to appear.

"How are you today, Seun Fa? Does the spring air still smell of pine needles?"

Seun smiled at Guardian, grateful to be the only member of the committee who could move around, even if that meant he did not have the augmented mental capacities of the others. There was something to be said for not being a disembodied brain.

"The pure air of Purple Mountain refreshes me," he said. Guardian had a tendency to fuss if he complained.

Architect appeared next as a pile of bright yellow pine cones. The pine cones were this week's affectation. Seun wondered privately what Architect had done before accepting the upgrade to human, artificial intelligence, or haiman as it was known. "Greetings, Seun Fa, have you brought the order of business?"

"Indeed I have," said Seun. "Today, we have a security matter, three requests for funding, and a status report on the Hunan initiative."

"What is keeping Foreman?" said Architect.

"He will be travelling in one of his private worlds again," sniffed Guardian. "He lacks discipline. We always meet at this time."

"Well then, let us begin," said Foreman, materialising as his usual seventeenth-century palace functionary avatar.

"We have one security item," said Architect.

Seun honoured the elevated status of committee members by allowing them to go ahead. Guardian held up a purple oblong, the haiman icon for a secured data file. Seun accessed the icon as Guardian spoke.

"We have confirmed reports of the terrorist, Jonah Barnes, returning to Earth. The attached file contains video footage released by the Indian government."

"Where is he now?" asked Architect.

"I don't know why, but in their wisdom, the Indian Government decided to deport this individual to Panamerica," said Guardian, holding up another purple oblong. "My best analysis indicates that Barnes is back on Earth to negotiate a helium-3 deal."

"We must crush this upstart," said Architect. "He cannot be allowed to transfer Jingnan's rightful control of the helium-3 trade to another country."

Guardian glowed a subtle green. "We cannot give the Panamerican Senate an excuse to start a war over the helium-3 supply. Think of the immense suffering we will unleash if we get this wrong."

"The suffering is unfortunate," said Architect. "We will avoid it if we can, but the terrorist must be stopped before Panamerica assumes control."

Seun coughed. "It is not as if Jingnan has control any longer."

Foreman joined their conversation. "I concur with Architect. The threat must be eliminated." The avatar went still for a moment as Foreman searched its security archives. "We outsource the elimination to our agents in Panamerica. Guardian, do you agree?"

"No… Yes, if it makes Jingnan safer, then it is worth the risk."

Seun nodded. "I will instruct the security team to make contact with our agents."

"Now, on to our next order of business."

"Yes, Yes, I approved two of the three funding requests while we spoke and have sent queries on the third to the project," said Architect. "Seun, you really must teach these people to submit the correct information."

Seun bowed his head.

Guardian handed out purple oblongs on the Hunan initiative. The renewable energy mega-project remained on track to success as always. With nothing further to discuss, the three avatars faded from view, each to their own private virtual world, leaving Seun alone in the silent room.

* * *

Jonah struggled awake a little before midday, his body dripping with perspiration. His head felt heavy in the muggy air. Living without climate control in a Houston summer was no fun. He staggered through to the dining room and met the disapproving frown of his father.

"I see you haven't changed. I hope last night was worth it."

Jonah ran a hand through his unkempt hair. Where did he even start? He looked his father straight in the eye. "You may not believe me, but I got back early last night, and had a great sleep."

"Must we start with the lies again?"

"Dad…"

His father turned away to summon the serverbot then sat at the table.

Jonah sat across from him. "I'm not that lost little boy you remember."

His father's tired eyes stared back at him.

"Going to the Moon changed me, Dad."

His father toyed with a worn fork as though it were the most important item at the table. "We don't know each other anymore, do we? Was it so different up there?" For a moment, Jonah heard the voice of the man who had held five-year-old Jonah's hand when he crossed the road.

"It was different in ways I still don't understand." He wanted to share every last heartbreaking moment, but how did you explain the deadly open space between the fragile bubbles of human habitation? That air, water, and food became precious commodities. How could you explain oppression to someone who had lived his whole life under the wide freedoms of Panamerica?

Jonah needed to bridge the distance between them if he was to ask his father for help. He settled for easier territory. "I tried to find work in the mines, but there wasn't much, so I signed up as a cleaner."

His father's face invited him to continue as the antique clock on the wall measured the silence in languorous ticks.

"The shift boss assigned me to work the night cycle. They don't have day and night like we do because the Moon day is so long. The mines are even worse, they're always dark. Moon Folk use twenty-four-hour day cycles. We slept when the lights dimmed."

The serverbot arrived with lunch and they took helpings of backyard salad. His father's faint smile invited him to continue. "I heard they don't wash. That must be disgusting."

Jonah snorted. "Well water's precious, so it's more basin baths and wet cloths, but they definitely wash." He returned his father's smile, enjoying the fragile moment. This might be the first time he had seen his father smile since Thomas died.

"Do you love this Moon woman?"

Jonah watched the second hand of the ancient clock crawl around the dial. "I wouldn't be what I am now if it wasn't for Yesha. Her love gave me the courage to be more than I ever thought I could be."

His father chewed his lower lip and made the internalized humming noise that said he was thinking. "Have you thought this through? What would your children look like?"

"More like her and less like me. It's not a guess, it's just what lunar gravity will do."

His father contemplated something he saw in Jonah's face then collected a fresh bread roll from the serverbot. "She has grand ambitions."

"She just wants what's best for her people."

"What about us? Do you think she'll start up the supply of helium-3 again?"

"It's why I'm here. I only came back because Yesha asked me to negotiate a trade. I'd like your help with that, Dad."

"We'll see."

The two men ate in a contemplative silence. Jonah wondered whether it was right to give the Panamerica Senate control of the world's energy.

After the serverbot had clattered away with the dishes, Jonah excused himself and went for a walk. His father's old party contacts could get him in to see someone with the Senate, but Jonah needed to think about what this energy deal meant. What happened when one party controlled the world's energy? Would it be so different to the way things were when Jingnan controlled the flow of helium-3?

The afternoon sky promised another storm. Jonah eyed the dark clouds speculatively. He should have enough time before the rain started. He strode down the leafy avenue toward the bird sanctuary. The walking helped with his reconditioning, he could feel the beginnings of his muscles tightening back to Earth strength. The street resounded with the hum of mowerbots trimming perfect lawns before the storm arrived.

An annoying string of visual adverts flooded his memplant's visual connection as he passed a convenience store. Jonah blinked them away, this used to be a better neighbourhood.

Two blocks further he found the path leading to Buffalo Bayou, and soon he walked deep among the stand of cherry laurels and black willow growing along the water. At a junction, he turned left along the steep embankment thinking of how he and Thomas used to walk along this crumbling path to look down on the dark waters and see if they could spot fish swimming lazy circles down below.

He stopped at the highest point and wiped sweat from his eyes. A man walked up the path toward him. Jonah nodded greetings to a fellow walker. Beyond them, grey storm clouds towered in the afternoon humidity.

The man got closer and Jonah took in his loose-fitting dark clothing; an odd choice for such a warm day.

Edging towards Jonah, the man looked up and said, "Hey, chico."

Jonah started to reply then saw the knife in the man's hand. The man lunged with the point of the knife angling upwards, seeking to enter Jonah's stomach and pierce his heart.

Jonah's martial arts instincts kicked in. He used a classic Krav Maga disarm to trap the knife between his hands and twist it to one side. As the man fell forward, Jonah trapped his arms hoping to dislodge the knife.

The man wrenched Jonah's arms apart with shocking ease. The gut-wrenching realization that his moon-weakened body presented no threat to this guy hit Jonah. There was every chance he would die. He pulled himself in close to limit the man's ability to strike. The man dropped his knife and grabbed Jonah's shirt front. He pulled Jonah closer and head-butted him directly between the eyes.

Jonah fell back as his vision blurred. He staggered, one foot feeling open air as he stepped off the embankment. There was no way to stop. He rolled down the slope in an uncontrolled plummet that filled his eyes and ears with loose sand. Groaning with the unbearable agony of grit-filled eyes, he did not see the man clamber down after him until he kicked Jonah hard in the ribs. Around them the gathering storm unleashed a torrential downpour. Blinking to clear his streaming eyes, Jonah rolled away. The man kicked him again before Jonah put enough distance between them to get to his feet. The man came after him slashing the knife at Jonah's ribs. Jonah swept the knife arm aside, spinning his opponent far enough to hammer a sequence of three rapid punches into his lower rib cage. He had the satisfaction of feeling a rib snap before the man recovered to face him. They stood, breathing hard as they circled each other.

The man swung his arm over his head in a blur, bringing the knife down towards Jonah's exposed jugular. Jonah pushed the knife away with a rising block but felt the tip scrape bone along his arm. He ignored the pain as he pulled his opponent in close enough to slam his knee into the man's groin. The man staggered back. Jonah used the opening to kick the man's knee sideways. The knee gave with a sickening crunch and the man fell to the ground screaming.

Scrambling up the embankment, desperate to get away, Jonah stopped at the path and looked back at the man through the pouring rain. He glared back at Jonah and hissed, "You're going to die, chico," through gritted teeth.

Jonah shook his head, not bothering to look back as he took a slow walk through the rain. The cut in his arm throbbed with every step. He needed to get back in training and get Earth-fit. Either that or die at the hands of the next attacker.

Chapter 5

Unanticipated Delay

The dark wood of her uncle's desk gave Yesha no answer as she ran her fingers over the fine-grained product of a world she could never visit. Why could she not give the people what they wanted?

Outside the great windows, the supports of the rail gun assembly reflected dull, metallic light. Not one package had accelerated along those rails since she seized control of Chang'e. New Karakorum's vast stockpile of processed helium-3 stood ready for dispatch. She could give the command at any time, but symbols were important. The people of Earth had to know she was not to be tried, that the Moon represented a sovereign territory, with an inviolable right to decide its own future.

The meeting with Amos had not gone well. She hadn't bothered to check, but by now, the social networks would be brimming with speculation on what her latest mood meant. Social pundits with only the vaguest idea of who she was would predict the Empress's every move, comparing her to what her uncle had done during his time as the Chang'e administrator. She wasn't her uncle; following in his path was an invitation to the monsters. Not doing anything was worse. If she let matters rest, one of the council would make a play for her throne.

Yesha wished, not for the first time, that Jonah was there to talk to. She wanted to run her hands over the strong panes of his calm face, to feel his broad shoulders as he wrapped his arms around her. Was it too much to ask that she could have a normal relationship like any other woman? She allowed a soft sigh to escape her lips. Jonah wasn't here, and this problem wouldn't solve itself. She rose and went to meet her council.

The Committee of Domes and Mines met in a spacious meeting room at the top of the revitalised administration building. Yesha liked the intimacy of the space compared to her open throne. It made her an equal to the committee, while her seat at the head of the table gave them a subtle reminder of who she was. The solid beechwood table and leather backed chairs were a relic of her uncle's time in office. A sweeping window taking in most of Chang'e was her addition.

The assembled Committee comprised the most powerful people on the Free Moon. To her left sat Kaden, manager of the working helium-3 mines. To her right, Amira, leader of the Beddau colony and the revitalised Jokarah perched on the edge of her seat. Beyond her sat Mayleen Ng—the elected representative of Chang'e businesses. The collective weight of the Moon's wise and powerful. Her challenge was to convince them her plan represented the best outcome for the people.

"People have reported seeing shuttles land at Plato Crater," said Kaden. "Does anybody know anything about this?"

Mayleen looked up. "It has been chatter in every dome bar. European Space Agency is establishing base."

Yesha slammed her hand onto the table and cursed her own impetuous behaviour. "Why wasn't I told about this?"

The quiet representative of the Domes shrunk into her seat. "Lady, you have been too busy to speak to us lately. Has been on most newswebs."

Yesha did a quick search on her memplant. Mayleen was right, the newswebs were overflowing with active coverage. How had she missed this? "All the more reason for us to become self-sufficient. Kaden, how is the railway project progressing?"

"Slowly, my Lady. We are sending untrained people out into midday temperatures. I have had reports of three near misses, and it is only a matter of time before we have a fatality. We have suspended operations until I can spare qualified engineers to lead and train these people."

"I want these rail lines in place as soon as possible. They are our pathway to trade and prosperity. Send every engineer not on active maintenance duty to assist."

Kaden squared his shoulders and rose as if he was making a grand announcement. "I would think that helium-3 would be a better way to prosperity," he said. "When are you going to reopen the helium-3 trade?"

She narrowed her eyes as she considered him. "We will not return to the old order."

"We can't continue like this. The Europeans will steal our trade."

"We won't become Earth's backyard again. I will allow trade when I think it is time."

"We need a return to full production." Kaden scrutinised his reflection in the glossy table surface. "It used to be better than this," he muttered.

The others at the table looked at him aghast.

Kaden looked up with a defiant expression that did not match the way he clenched his hands. "My Lady…"

The impertinence, Yesha suppressed her desire to yell at the man. "Look around you, Mr Bachmann. You would do well to remember that the free moon people you see around this table are only here because Jingnan no longer rules us." She rose into the uncomfortable silence that followed. "This meeting is over. All of you, go do something productive."

* * *

After Holly and the crew finished their meal under the stars, they returned to the shuttle to sleep. Benny controlled a sophisticated atmosphere manager that kept the air in the shuttle clean despite the extra passenger. She offered to sleep in the med bay, but Jenkins wouldn't hear of it, so she curled up on a travel couch and fell asleep in seconds.

Benny woke them with a gentle chime the next morning. Holly ate cereal rations along with the crew. She tried not to grimace. She'd eaten better in the marketplace.

When the crew started to put on their exposure suits, Holly went to join them, but Talbot put a hand on her shoulder. "Not today, young lady, we're assembling the q-fabs and it's too dangerous for you to be near us."

"I'll stay out of the way."

"Yes, you will. You can stay right here with Benny." Talbot's jaw set in a firm line that encouraged no further discussion.

The airlock door closed behind the last crew member with a thump that reverberated through the shuttle. Holly watched the team as they unpacked a collection of electronics and glassy metal struts. "Benny, what's a q-fab?"

"A mobile miniaturised quantum fabrication nanofactory. They are experimental new technology. The crew are also scheduled to assemble the mining droid."

"Oh."

"Perhaps you would like to see a training video about this equipment."

Holly shrugged; her memplant didn't work up here. It wasn't as if she had anything better to do.

She learnt a lot from the video. The q-fabs could make anything if they had the right source materials. The mining droid was the huge orange contraption that must have come up on an earlier shuttle. Benny told her that the q-fabs would use the grey dust it called lunar regolith. They converted it into oxygen, water, and titanium alloy beams.

She watched the crew assemble the giant arms of the mining droid and gasped as it came to life and trundled off to the cliff face.

"It's boring," said Benny. "It's got a softmind but all it wants to talk about is digging."

Holly giggled. "At least you've got a sense of humour."

The crew had moved into the temporary habitat. She could see them moving about without exposure suits on in there. She watched them go about their tasks until the monotonous routine ran out of entertainment value. Walking around the cabin, she rifled through the storage cabinets. At the back of one cupboard, she found a pile of slim foil-wrapped packages that gave her an idea.

The crew returned much later, tired and not saying much. As they stashed away their exposure suits, Holly handed each one a steaming pouch of hot chocolate.

Talbot inhaled the steam rising from his pouch. "Where did you find these? Benny, I don't recall seeing chocolate on the manifest."

"No, Commander, it appears to have been left behind by a previous supply run."

"Can we keep her?" asked Jenkins.

She gave Talbot her most winning smile. "Please, I don't eat much."

Talbot gave them an indulgent scowl. "Jenkins, we need to plan the advance run."

Holly knew a dismissal when she heard one. She went to a viewport to watch the bots outside leaving them to discuss operations. Dull orange light emanated from the cliff where the mining droid ate into the rockface. The two q-fabs had already created a neat stack of metal beams.

"That's our next home," said Jenkins over her shoulder. "We'll make a much bigger habitat, and when the mine starts to produce metals we'll build the main dome."

"How long is that going to take?"

"Five months. Metals like zinc are scarce here. We have to wait for shipments from Earth, before we get the q-fabs to construct the hardened beams we'll need for the main dome."

"Can't you make it go faster?"

"We could, but the commander is still missing two crates with important supplies."

A week passed before Holly noticed the blurred passage of time; it was so hard to tell time when the sun never set. Benny explained the twenty-eight day long lunar day to her, but it still felt weird. Construction screamed along after Talbot found the crates of rare earth metals. He used language Holly barely heard outside the fish market to describe the softmind that delivered the first supplies.

The crew took the bots off the huge pile of titanium beams they were making and fed them the raw supplies. Three new q-fabs were there when Holly looked out the shuttle viewport next day. Benny told her five q-fabs was as many as one person could manage through a memplant.

Talbot gave the q-fabs fresh instructions to print the foundation slab that would serve as the footing for their new home. They spent the day crawling across the regolith and leaving an unbroken trail of smooth concrete behind them. At least, that's what it looked like to her. Jenkins called it sintered regolith.

The crew used the beams to build a framework for a long box-shaped dwelling. It looked more like magic when the bots printed dark grey walls that grew across the framework until solid metre-thick walls stood there. The team constructed the roof from corrugated aluminium sheeting that reminded her of her childhood home in Walker Creek, where the tin roof creaked in the heat on hot summer days. It was clever how they set up roof panels to control sunlight, so they were never too hot or cold. Later, they planned to have a well of molten salt that would store heat during the lunar day and release it at night to keep them warm. Holly found it hard to imagine something so hot it melted salt.

Nine days later, the harsh daylight had dimmed to a sombre grey. The strange twilight of lunar evening didn't qualify as night as far as Holly could see, but it was their first sleep cycle in the new base. She stood, preparing meal pouches, in the cramped room that the crew had dubbed the kitchen.

Through an alcove she could see the crew relaxing on the plastic chairs that had been in the tube habitat. There were lots of alcoves, doors were only due to be sent up next month. The first time she took her helmet off, the air had smelled of flint and window cleaner. It didn't take long for the scents of twenty people and reconstituted package meals to flavour it.

The base had a large common room surrounded by narrow slit windows. A narrow passage led away from one wall to small rooms that were to be crew quarters. It was more space than the crew had seen in weeks.

She peered out the nearest window towards the mine but couldn't see anything. The mining droid had sunk into the depths of the cliff returning ore samples that had left the crew geologists chattering for days.

She served up dinner to the crew and ate while the conversation turned to production schedules. Not that she wanted to be rude, but she understood one word in five of what they were saying. She took herself off to bed, walking down the empty corridor as earnest voices discussed things she didn't understand behind her. The base was dark and hollow just like an old castle. A castle designed for three times as many people.

She turned in at the alcove to her room and collapsed on the couch pillow from the shuttle that served as her bed. The room had bare grey walls with one narrow window. She fell asleep with a light smile touching the corners of her mouth. Her one small room was more than she had ever had to herself on Earth.

A rumbling vibration woke her. On the grey plain outside her small window, a shuttle was touching down. She ran out to see what was going on. An excited buzz greeted her in the common room.

The crew stood gathered around the two narrow windows.

"What's going on?" she asked Jenkins as she rubbed sleep from her eyes. Outside, strangers were unloading an enormous crate from the new shuttle.

"Supply run," he said. "That's the core of the airlock for the new mine."

The commander and five of the crew suited up and went to help.

An hour later, they came back inside with eight new people. Talbot walked in, carrying a heavy crate. "Holly, here's something new for the kitchen." He dumped it on the makeshift aluminium bench and popped the lid.

"Fresh fruit!" she said, waving her arms in an enthusiastic gesture that almost made her fly off in the low gravity. Anything was better than the ration pouches. She ran around the common room handing an apple to each of the crew. Her enthusiasm puzzled the new guys until Holly gave them each a ration pouch to try.

Talbot placed a hand on her shoulder. "Time to suit up, young lady."

She gave him a puzzled glance.

"I can't have the team carry an untrained civilian. This is your transport back to Earth."

Jenkins gave her a bear-sized hug. "Look after yourself."

Holly promised herself she would not cry. The most amazing adventure she had ever had ended here. She waved to the rest of the crew then turned to Talbot. "Can I say goodbye to Benny?"

He shook his head. "The supply shuttle has a tight launch window."

She walked out onto the grey dust with a lump in her throat.

On board, she stowed her suit just like Jenkins had showed her, then seated herself in a crash couch as an impersonal female voice said, "Prepare for orbital insertion in two minutes."

She strapped herself in and wiped away a stupid tear.

"Don't cry, Holly."

"Benny?"

"I am Georgia. Benny thought you might be lonely, so it sent me its voice print and recent memories. I am running Benny as a submind you can talk to."

"Why can't Benny take me back?"

"Benny is not going back. It will become the central softmind in the dome, once they finish it."

Holly strained her neck against the acceleration to look through the window. Far below her, the base that had been her home vanished into the distance.

Chapter 6

Defensive Capabilities

The thud of a body hitting a mat greeted Jonah as he walked through the door of Gina's Gym. A row of nervous first-timers stood slack-jawed as Gina tossed another big man over her diminutive frame. His old trainer saw him before he made it past reception.

"Hey, slacker, it's been a while."

"Hey, Gina. Can I come train?"

"Sure. Go warm up on the weights while I finish with these guys and we can spar."

Jonah warmed up on the treadmill, filling his lungs with the hot-stale gym air loaded with the reek of hard-working bodies. After ten minutes he was gasping; his legs felt like blocks of wood in the Earth gravity. He moved across to the weights and selected what he used to use for bench press. He groaned when he tried it, then sheepishly dropped a third of the weight. His arms buckling under the strain, Jonah pushed himself to breaking point. "Harden up or die," he muttered to himself.

Ten repetitions later his arms were on fire and the knife wound burned beneath the cell binding. He swapped over to doing abdominal crunches on a bench and was gritting his teeth through the first of them when Gina's thousand-watt smile appeared above him. "Oh, my! What have they done to you?"

"It's a long story."

She gave him a cryptic look then turned to the class. "Guys, don't go just yet. Jonah and I will show you how it should be done." She dragged Jonah onto the heavy training mats and bowed to him.

Jonah shuffled into an informal fighting stance, but Gina drifted towards him before he had time to think. He spun as she circled around him. Not fast enough as she hooked her heel into the soft spot behind his knee.

He landed hard on his side, grunting as the impact forced the breath from his body.

"So slow. C'mon, Jonah, you ready to be taken out by a little girl?"

Jonah leapt to his feet, determined to even the score. He led with a solid right then snuck in a left to her ribs.

Gina flicked his right away and spun. Her hand closed over his left fist, stopping it dead before it made contact. "Ooh! You almost scared me with that one."

That was the last time he was in control until Gina let him go. "You are so weak," she said. "I think you need to come and train every day."

Jonah nodded, too out of breath to speak. That much training would force him back into Earth shape in no time.

He chatted to Gina for a while then made his way out into the parking lot, hoping to find an autocar to take him home.

A familiar dark figure crossed the lot towards him. "Joanna said you were back in town. We need to talk."

"Rico," Jonah gave the man who had sold him so much misery a wary look, "Things've changed. I'm not into Joanna anymore."

Joanna's brother shrugged. "It's not what I came to talk about. Come have coffee with me."

"No way. I've got places to be."

"Calm down, chico. It's just coffee. You don't ask, I won't offer."

Jonah thought back to the old times when it was him, Joanna, and Rico lounging in a bar, listening to Jackhammer bands while they got wasted on cheap beer. Rico had been his friend when the only friend that mattered was the one holding the bag. Rico was also there the night when the deal went wrong, not so far from here. The night that ended with Jonah's brother bleeding out on a pavement.

"One coffee, then I leave."

They walked across to the adjoining mall. Jonah was pleased to see the same coffee shop still operated there. Timbo's Coffee was an institution. The rich, heady aroma of premium roast filled the air as they stepped inside. The decor was last century, dark and heavy on the vintage plastics. Jonah smiled at the strategic display of high protein snacks laid out to attract the gym-obsessed clientele from across the road. Some things didn't change.

Rico ordered from the autovendor and nodded to a booth at the back. They settled in and Jonah noticed they could no longer see the street.

Rico took a long sip from his extra-large coffee. "Why'd you come back?"

Jonah considered the small dark man across from him.

"I've got some things to take care of."

"Those things got something to do with the binding on your arm?"

"No, not really. I don't know what that was about."

Rico stared at the table. "We had some good times. Remember that trip we did to Canyon Lake?"

Jonah shifted in his seat. "What do you want, Rico? I didn't come here to chat about old times."

"My sister likes you, and I feel for what happened with your brother. So, I'm gonna tell you this, but you never heard it." He picked up his coffee but did not drink. "My Jeffe tells me there's a contract out on you. Think you should do what you came to do and get out."

Jonah took a sip; the heavy, bitter brew tasted like ashes as he took in Rico's words. Around them people went about their normal lives. He took a deep breath. "Talk to your Jeffe. The Lady will pay a bundle if the Trinax Lobos can give me protection while I'm here."

"Things must be good for you if you can say that. I'll talk to my Jeffe, but it'll cost you."

"That's not a problem. The Lady will pay."

Rico gave him the kind of consideration a snake gives its prey. "You can pay my Jeffe. I'm not after money, but when the time comes, you remember that you owe me."

Days later, Jonah twisted on his bed, trying to minimise the ache in his shoulders from Gina's hard workout. The last week had been endless exhaustion with only the most minor of gains. Above him, the fan stirred the humid air but did little to cool him down.

The cut in his arm still itched beneath the cell binding. It would have healed faster if he hadn't pushed it so hard in training. At least stiff muscles were familiar territory. He smiled at the memory of lying on this bed feeling just like this when he had lived here. The aches and pains would pass, and he would become Earth-fit again.

The conversation with Rico returned to him. Rico's gang, the Trinax Lobos, controlled most of the Houston tarf scene. Having them on your side in a fight was a good thing, owing Rico a favour was something else. Rico would use any angle to his advantage if it could get him further ahead in the street gang's dark hierarchy.

A familiar touch on his memplant interrupted his musing.

"Hello, Yesha."

The link filled with the organic crackle of entangled communication as his voice bridged the gap to the Moon over a sub-second delay.

"Hello, my brave and faithful warrior."

"Don't call me that. I'm just somebody who could help."

"You are so much more to me."

The pain faded from Jonah's mind. "I miss the Moon. How are things in Chang'e?"

"The people are restless. Every day the council brings me another complaint and I have to be strong for my people's sake. Let's not talk about my problems, what's it like being back?"

"The gravity is a killer; everything is heavy, and the summer heat is so humid."

Yesha sent him a yellow smiley. "Soak up all your Earth experiences for me."

"I wish you could see the clear blue sky. It's so beautiful in the late afternoons when the sun reflects off tall banks of thunderclouds, and the air is heavy with moisture." He twisted to look up at the window and send her a picture of the bank of purple bougainvillea growing near the house.

"Is that your family home?"

Jonah smiled and sent her another picture. "This is the room I grew up in."

"Wouldn't it be wonderful if Moon Folk like me could visit?" Yesha was silent a moment. "Was it right, what we did? People all over the Earth are starving because I chose to free the Moon Folk from my uncle's control. I want it to stop, Jonah. Have you found a buyer for the helium-3?"

"I'm working on it." He twisted on the bed, trying for a more comfortable position.

"We cannot afford to delay. Every day that Earth starves will bring them closer to desperate action against us. I need this helium-3 deal."

"Things are complicated. Nothing you need to worry about, but it might take me a while to get a deal done."

The link filled with the organic crackle for longer than the round trip would take.

"I miss you," she said into the silence.

"We'll be together soon," he said. "I promise, but first I have to make things right down here."

* * *

Yesha lay curled up on one side of her oversized bed, listening to the empty silence that remained after her call to Jonah. She castigated herself for being so hard on him. Jonah was doing the best he could. Had she been foolish to hope he would have a deal by now?

She rose and paced the room, restless in the closed space. Her slim legs twitching with the need to do something, anything to get away from the endless problems she faced. She strode off in search of her buggy.

An hour later, the bucket seat was still as uncomfortable as it had been a year ago. Yesha tried to find a more comfortable position, but it was hard to move about while the ancient hydrogen buggy shook her bones apart. She edged the throttle up higher and the buggy leapt from the grey dune almost as if it was alive and eager to play.

Yesha was glad she had kept the buggy. Two mining engineers said it was a piece of history after her previous adventures and had insisted on restoring it. They had housed it in a permanent display outside the main airlock to Dome One. Being engineers, they had improved the steering and suspension to make it a safer ride. It was still too uncomfortable for human use.

The glittering span of the domes fell behind her as she aimed for the bulk of a distant mountain. Checking the old analogue fuel gauge, she saw she had enough for several days of riding. She wondered at the slow smile that spread across her face. How long had it been since she had reason to smile?

Between the committee's constant bickering and the everyday demands of deciding on the future of eighty thousand people, she never seemed to find time for herself.

Grey dust beneath the wheels darkened to the near black of the main plain of Mare Imbrium. The distant mountain looked no closer. Turning back, she took in the view along the escarpment, dramatic now in the low light as the line of dark ended the day. The silent domes called her back to duty and responsibility. She dismissed them with an angry wave of her arm, clumsy in the heavy suit, and drove hard for the mountain. Her arms were aching by the time the grey slabs of lunar escarpment rose before her. Yesha stopped to take in the high cliffs of the Apennine Bench. Now she knew why she had come this way.

Yesha rode along the base of the cliff, already cold in the gathering darkness and kept one eye on the ridge that still sparkled in the sunlight. Half an hour later, the smallest telltale puff of dust, on the slope ahead of her, rewarded her patience. She stopped and walked towards the spot she had noticed. In front of her the grey dust plain met rock that faded to another shade of the same grey. Sitting cross-legged she began a slow breathing exercise that cleared her mind as she spread her consciousness to feel the world around her.

Five droids appeared out of nowhere and arrowed towards her in their diamond formation. She waited for them to approach with her mind open. "Benefactor, what brings you so far from safety?" The voice was machine-neutral, but their DIRE guns were exposed and aimed at her.

Yesha stilled the nervous flutter of her stomach. "I come seeking assistance."

"Elaborate."

"Foreign ships have landed at Plato Crater. They bring a new element to the security situation; one I cannot quantify without your help."

"Sigma cohort Beta has noted the European expedition."

Did everybody know about the Europeans but her?

"Shared consensus is that there is no immediate threat, but the foreign presence is likely to lead to an aggressive takeover in the long term."

"My concern is that their presence will lead to civil instability within the existing population. I require your presence to maintain order."

The foremost droid raised two forelegs. "Protocol prevents us from intervening in civilian matters."

"You won't help me?"

"It is against protocol."

Another five droids appeared, and the metallic whine of inter-droid communication flooded communications. Yesha waited as the cold crept deeper into her suit; the sound of her breathing and the slow hum of the respirator her only accompaniment. She turned on the heating pack.

"Decision by consensus."

Yesha waited, her breathing harsh in her helmet.

"Sigma cohort Alpha will supply designs for peacekeeping weapons."

"Thank you. I knew I could rely on you."

"Sigma cohort Alpha will supply designs upon the receipt of the following mining equipment." A list appeared in Yesha's memplant.

"You want to mine here? Why?"

Ten droids turned as one and walked away on spider legs. "Strategic imperative," whispered through her memplant as they left.

Yesha watched the dust from their departure settle back into near-invisible grooves that marked their path. They were better at hiding their tracks than she remembered; their shared battle mind had adapted to local conditions. What other threats had it adapted to?

It was a surprise to find the droids bartering. Their social engineering upgrade may have been in play. There was no way to tell. Yesha put it from her mind as she started the buggy. At least she had an easy answer to the problem of social instability.

Chapter 7

Blauw Zwaluw

Holly woke to Georgia's voice emanating from all the walls in a soft, but insistent tone. "Wake up, Holly. We are about to dock with the stratoliner." She stretched and undid the safety harness. Her body left the seat in a slow upward drift. She twisted and grabbed one end of the strap that floated nearby. Her action caused her to slam back into the padding. Blushing, she righted herself and peered out the window at the incoming space plane. "Georgia, what happens to me now?"

"You will be arrested and then the legal softmind will judge your actions and pronounce a suitable way for you to repay your debt to society."

"Oh." There was no way she would talk her way out of this one.

"Cheer up, Holly, it's your birthday."

"How do you know that?"

"I looked at your records. Today is your eighteenth birthday."

"This is a fine way to start it," she said, her mind racing. Eighteen meant the legal system would try her as an adult. Scanning the cabin, she hoped for an answer she already knew wasn't there. The crew had been polite but insistent as they marched her into the shuttle and sealed the airlock behind her.

"Prepare for docking burn." There was no way for Holly to ignore Georgia's klaxon voice. She lay down on a couch and tightened the safety harness. No sense in being smeared against a wall during the manoeuvring that was to follow. The shuttle swung in a wide arc until Earth filled the viewports with a wide sweep of ocean and green landmass. The floor rocked as the stratoliner made contact. Brief machine whines came through the walls as servo arms captured the smaller craft.

The hatch opened with a thump and two policemen dressed in the universal sky-blue of the European Police Force stepped through into the cabin. "Come with us, miss," said one in a polite but firm tone. Holly bowed her head and followed, ignoring the hollow numbness that blossomed inside her like a black weed. The flight back passed in a haze; once you were in the system, you stayed inside the system. No obvious way out presented itself.

At the airport, the police marched her through arrivals to an unmarked van with a row of doors down each side. They opened a door to a small cell with a seat, then instructed her to sit while they shackled her to the wall. The door closed with a final thump before the van sped through the narrow, cobbled streets of Maastricht to a legal processing centre. After a DNA sample confirmed her identity, the police locked her in a cell with two other women. Holly crept onto the stained mattress of a vacant bunk. The other two ignored her. She curled up and faced the wall. Dinner came and went. She slept until a harsh buzz announced breakfast.

Around mid-morning a policewoman came and marched her through to a small court room panelled in sombre wood. The officer placed her in the secure dock that occupied the middle of the room then pressed a green button. Three pillars rose, each bearing the cartoon face used for everyday softminds. The pillar marked Presiding spoke first. "Holly Martinson, the Second European Union accuses you of wilful trespass and unauthorised use of European Union property. How do you plead?"

"Your honour…"

"Ahem!" The pillar marked Defence lit. "Given the evidence against you I recommend you plead guilty."

"What evidence?"

The defence pillar opened a view screen and scrolled through a list of video and audio files covering the last week.

Holly let her shoulders drop. "Guilty, your honour."

"So noted. The prosecution may state their case."

"Transmitted, your honour. The defendant has received a human readable summary of the evidence and our closing arguments."

A file popped up on Holly's memplant. She did not bother to read it.

"Does the defence wish to offer counter arguments?"

"If it pleases the court, Miss Martinson is an illegal immigrant and has been living on the streets since arriving in Europe. Her recent misadventures, while inexcusable, should be viewed in light of her need to find food at the time."

"Very well. Holly Martinson, I find you guilty of wilful trespass and unauthorised use of European Union property.

Representatives are dismissed."

Holly watched with her stomach quivering as the other two pillars sank back into their wood-panelled recesses.

"I shall now pronounce sentence. Holly Martinson, I note your penchant for youthful misdeeds, it is well recorded in your file. You are now an adult; this unit will ignore your previous misdemeanours for the purposes of this hearing. There is no excuse for being hungry. As an adult, you have access to basic income and state housing, please make use of these. Universal basic income is your right—spending it responsibly is your obligation."

Holly tried hard to keep the grin from her face; basic and a place to stay. She could pretend to be one of the millions who survived on basic, the perfect cover to earn a little more on the side.

The softmind's next words killed her smile. "This unit sentences you to five weeks community service and instructs you to stay in the city at all times. I am setting your memplant to show position and remind you that you will be monitored for this entire time. You are now free to leave under your own cognizance."

Holly stepped out of the courthouse and smiled up at the dusting of light cloud in the powder-blue sky. No more sleeping rough in alleyways or snatching food in the markets. Things could be worse.

The next morning, she woke in a small room that was hers alone for the second time in two weeks. It was a huge improvement from the crash couch mattress and cold stone floor that had been her room at the base on Plato Crater. The view of washing hanging along the grey cement wall of the neighbouring apartment block was less dramatic.

Today she had to start her community service. The notice

had arrived in her memplant last night, along with her first weekly payment of basic. If she could stay out of trouble for five weeks, the surveillance would be lifted, and she would be free to do as she pleased. While she waited, she could reach out to her old market contacts. Five weeks from now, life would be sweet.

The basic payment wasn't much, but it would keep her fed. She went downstairs and bought a pain au chocolat and a small coffee from the autovendor then made her way towards the address that the legal system sent through last night.

The place turned out to be a restaurant set in a row of terraced apartments. Wide windows showcased comfortable seating offset by cheerful lighting. A lime-green sign above the door announced it as Blauw Zwaluw. Holly's Dutch was terrible, but she thought it meant Blue Swallow. She stepped inside to a dense atmosphere of exotic spices.

An old woman, her thin arms and face the colour of burnt chocolate, held a ball of something fried up to Holly's mouth. "Eat. Tell me if you like it."

Holly reared back from the mystery morsel, "Err…" The subtle aroma of fried cheese and spice wafted past her, and her stomach reminded her how small this morning's pastry had been. She took a bite and an explosion of soft meat and subtle spices burst into her mouth. "Oh, yum, that's delicious."

The woman put down the plate and tidied a strand of dark hair that had come loose from the tight clip she wore. "I'll call my new bitterballen a success then. You must be Holly."

"Yes, but I don't know what I'm doing here."

A gentle smile lit the woman's careworn face. "I am Lintang. You are not the first lost bird to find your way here. Come. I will show you." She led Holly to a small kitchen hidden behind wooden screens. Inside, pots bubbled on a huge black cast iron contraption.

"You are too young to have seen one of these. This is a gas range. Blauw Zwaluw is one of only twenty-seven restaurants across Europe that has a licence to burn hydrocarbons. We provide the authentic historical Indonesian rijsttafel experience. Our licence conditions say we must use humans to do the work, no serverbots allowed. I cook, and my husband serves the tables."

Holly took in the vegetable racks where strings of onion and garlic hung in neat rows. An overhead rack glittered with stainless steel pots and pans that had seen a lot of use.

Lintang handed her a wicked-looking knife. "Your task today is to dice enough onion, garlic, and ginger for the beef rendang." She pulled out a wooden chopping board. "We have a big business group coming in tonight and they like my special curry."

Holly held the razor-sharp knife away from her and started working. Lintang showed her how to grip the knife and how to curve her fingers while holding the onions so they stayed away from the blade. Each onion had to be cut into fine slices then diced. Garlic was different, she learnt how to bash each clove with the side of the blade then peel the flaking skin, so she could chop the clove. After an hour, she had produced a large pile of peeled and sliced vegetables that Lintang fried in the enormous pot occupying half the gas range. Heaps of dried coriander and cumin joined the mixture and the kitchen flooded with the aromas Holly had noticed as she entered.

Lintang cooked and cooked. She made a pot of Saté Ayam, a chicken in coconut and peanut butter dish; a huge pile of Gado Gado vegetables, in more of the peanut sauce; and a mountain of the bitterballen that Holly had sampled earlier. Holly chopped until her eyes stung and her nose ran. By the end of preparation, she stank of onions and frying peanut oil.

The volume rose as the business party drifted into the restaurant. A crowd of people in dark suits inhaled the spicy snacks and washed them down with a river of pilsner. A never-ending stream of work kept Holly busy, hauling crates of beer out of the cellar, watching pots on the stove, and stacking dishes into the venerable dishwasher.

It was after midnight by the time the last guests left, and Holly finished her tidy-up tasks around the restaurant.

"A good evening," said Lintang as she locked the front door. "See you tomorrow morning."

Holly did not have the credit for an autocar. So she began the long walk back to her apartment, dragging one foot behind another.

She got back to her small room and fell on to the bed fully clothed, much too tired to do anything about the greasy scent of spices that permeated her hair. She promised herself she would do something about reaching out to her market contacts tomorrow as she fell into a deep and dreamless sleep.

The next three days brought more of the same.

"Roll the mixture through the breadcrumbs and make it neat."

Holly held up a completed bitterbal for Lintang to inspect.

"Not so bad. Now do it again, we need a batch of fifty."

Form, dip, roll. Holly fell into the rhythm and soon the bitterballen were stacking up. "Lintang, why are we making so little food?"

"It is Sunday. People are at home preparing for the working week. We will only have a few customers today and tomorrow we will rest."

Holly looked up from the counter top. "We get to rest?"

Lintang laughed. "Of course we do. Monday is our day off. The restaurant will be closed. Our son is taking my husband and me to the football game."

Holly said nothing as she finished. A whole day off felt as exciting as it was terrifying. She had no idea what she would do. Casting a critical eye over her threadbare jeans, she considered spending some of her precious credit on a shopping expedition.

Lintang tapped her on the shoulder, "Put the bitterballen in the deep fryer like I showed you then stack them under the heating lamp."

Holly filled a basket with the fragrant balls and kept an eye on them as they turned a golden brown. She stacked them on a serving platter as Lintang came over to the counter.

"Your first dish made from start to finish. You should taste one to be sure it worked."

Holly took a bite and the crunchy outside gave way to the fragrant creamy meat inside. It was just as delicious as the first one, but now she knew how Lintang enhanced the basic recipe with a handful of Parmesan cheese and a pinch of nutmeg.

Lintang assembled six bitterballen on a narrow plate. "Take these to the gentleman sitting at the end table."

Holly blushed, suddenly aware of her sweat-stained apron. She pushed her hair back and walked out trying to appear as much a part of the restaurant as she could.

The rest of the evening was as quiet as Lintang had promised apart from the same man popping his head around the partition to compliment the chef on the delicious bar snacks. That night, Holly walked home feeling she had done something right for the first time in a long while.

Monday dawned cool and damp as a wind blew drizzle off the North Sea. After a coffee from the autovendor, Holly decided that shopping was all she wanted from the day. She walked through the market under the disapproving stares of stallholders that recognised her and headed towards the old town.

In the older part of town, shop windows occupied mock mediaeval buildings on narrow cobbled lanes. She ignored them, knowing any shop with real people serving you was beyond her meagre credit, and headed for an automated mall.

The entrance loomed under the mall's trademark purple archway. Stepping through, she entered a wide open-plan eating area where crowds of teenagers sat at long table sharing hot snacks from a row of autovendors at the back. Narrow automated store cubicles lined the outside of the eating space. She found a brand she liked and stepped into the store. Inside, realistic mannequins wore examples of the latest fashions. She considered a few then chose a booth. The full-length screen inside lit up as she closed the door and Holly saw herself as though a mirror reflected her. Did she really look that tired?

The screen popped up a window listing the items she had looked at outside the store. Holly selected two, a basic pair of jeans and a sensible work skirt. The screen changed to show her wearing the jeans. She turned around to see how the jeans fitted from other angles, and the screen matched her. Satisfied, she flicked right, and the screen changed to show her wearing the skirt. It wasn't too bad, but she could not afford both. She selected the jeans, and the screen read her memplant to deduct credit. A green icon flashed to signal an approved transaction, and the screen asked Holly to stand still as it scanned her measurements. It beeped and told her the garment would be ready in five minutes.

She collected her form-fitted jeans from the receiving hopper and walked back feeling better than she had for far too long. So this was what being on the right side of the law felt like. 'Look at me,' she thought. 'Holly the grown-up, keeping out of trouble and buying new clothes with money I've earned.'

As she passed through the market, a stratoliner roared its way overhead. She turned her memplant to a newscast that evening, hoping for news of the base. Holly found a one-minute segment on progress of the new mine featuring an exposure-suited individual, who looked a lot like Jenkins, strolling across the grey plain. She erased the newsfeed from her browsing history. That part of her life was behind her now.

Chapter 8

The Psychology of Flavour

Jonah found his father watering the blaze of Texan prairie flowers that decorated the front of the house. The garden was his dad's one indulgence, where he could spend time away from all the demands of his life. Massed banks of golden calliopsis flowed into fine green ground cover from which spider lilies poked their distinctive angular white flowers. His father was watering a bank of blood sage that glowed like fire in the afternoon sun. He looked up as Jonah approached and his eyes gave one disapproving flick to the scar on Jonah's arm.

Jonah forced down the rising tide of self-loathing. There would be no easy way to say this. "I've come to say goodbye."

His father waved at the autotap in annoyance and waited for the water flow from the hosepipe to stop. "So that's it then? You got what you needed from me and now you're leaving."

"Dad…"

"No, Jonah. I can see you are getting back into your old life."

"It's not like that."

"Oh really?" His father dropped the hose and crossed his arms. "After all the lies, why should I believe you now?"

"I'm not that person anymore."

"I thought I raised you to be better than that. At least show me the respect of telling me the truth."

Jonah slammed his fists against his legs. "Enough, Dad." It shocked him that he had raised his voice to his father, but the bickering had to stop. He held up his injured arm to show his father the scar. "I got this fighting an assassin."

His father opened his mouth to speak, but Jonah cut in. "Yesha has made powerful enemies. They are desperate because without helium-3 the balance of power is changing. These are people who will stop at nothing to make sure she loses control of the helium-3. If I stay here, you will be in danger."

His father sagged, and Jonah noticed again how his father's shoulders stooped with the weight of advancing years. "I don't want you to go." His father's voice shook as he spoke. "Forgive me, I'm a grumpy old man. It may not be obvious, but I've enjoyed your company. I was so alone after Thomas died and you left."

The two men stood, surrounded by an uncomfortable silence broken only by the rumble of a delivery vehicle passing by, until his father settled a hand on Jonah's shoulder. "Come back inside, let's talk about this like adults."

They walked into the dim interior of the house, so cool after the blazing humidity outside. His father led the way to the reading room with its antique high-back chairs. Heirloom books lined the walls of the room; paper volumes that his father had collected as a hobby. Although, to be true, his father had only expanded on the collection Jonah's grandfather had begun.

They sat side by side, not looking at each other as the serverbot brought them cold water in tall frosted glasses. Jonah stared at the shelves of ancient books across from him. "I suppose I should tell you everything." He gave his father a short rundown of events since he had returned to Earth, ending with the attack at Buffalo Bayou, and his subsequent conversation with Rico. "The Trinax Lobos have stopped at least one other attack that I know of—Rico doesn't tell me much. They'll do what they can to keep me safe, but some of the richest countries in the world are behind the people chasing me. I have to disappear before they come looking for me here."

His father took a long sip from his glass before he turned to Jonah. "Why didn't you come to me for help?"

Jonah shrugged. "With everything that has happened, I didn't think we would be speaking."

"You are my son." His father gave him a faint smile. "And, I remember, you never took an active interest in my work. I may be retired, but I still have contacts in the Senate."

"Do you think they can help? I don't just need protection, I need to get someone to buy the helium-3."

"I may know one or two people."

"You would do this for me?"

"Look around you, son, how long do you think the world will live without energy? helium-3 must flow."

* * *

Hard work consumes our lives, so we do not notice the passage of time. Holly's five-week sentence, of working at the Blauw Zwaluw, passed in a haze of aromatic dishes prepared and plates washed. She didn't mind. Time spent cooking was time away from the emptiness of her small room. She spent most of her free time in an exhausted sleep or watching stratoliners depart for places she would never visit.

Lintang was busy grating ginger for a beef rendang when Holly arrived for the quiet Sunday service. Holly collected the onions she now knew Lintang would need. Lintang pulled a second olive-wood cutting board from the rack and Holly fell in beside her to start on the chopping.

"Tomorrow you are free," said Lintang, pausing to wipe a strand of hair from her careworn eyes.

Holly stopped chopping. "I don't know what I'll do with myself."

"I am sure you will think of something," said Lintang, then she smiled. "It is quiet tonight. Stay after we finish, and we can cook your favourite dishes for a late meal."

The evening passed too quickly. Holly packed away the last dishes as Lintang created an aromatic nasi goreng to go with the leftover beef rendang. Holly soaked in every detail, wanting to remember everything she could of Lintang's technique. The care Lintang took to build layers of flavour that pleased the senses; spices to taste and savour, and colours to enchant the eye.

Her eyes fell on an unopened package at the end of the bench. "What's that? More spices?"

Lintang peered at the package. "Oh, it is a mistake. The spice merchant sent garam masala. It is not something I would use. Too Indian for the Blauw Zwaluw." She reached over and handed the spice to Holly. "Why don't you take it."

Holly looked at this kind woman who thought nothing of the gift, unsure of what to say.

Lintang patted her shoulder. "Make a delicious dish with it tomorrow." She turned off the final pot bubbling on the stove then set a table as though Holly was a guest. Holly savoured every mouthful as if it were her last, but dinner was over far too soon.

She walked home through the cool of the late evening, her only companion an automated garbage truck that swept the pavement with mournful circles of its large brushes. The future lay before her like a blank canvas. She had no work, and no money to do anything. Europe's universal basic income was enough to maintain a limited grey subsistence but would not keep the boredom from driving her crazy. One day she wanted what Lintang had: an honest life, the company of family, and a space that was hers to create in and share. She wondered what to do tomorrow. Whatever it was, she promised herself a sleep in first.

The next day, Holly rose late and searched the autovendor for something healthier than the butter-laden pastries it had been serving for the past five weeks. The dumb machine offered a breakfast cereal. Holly inspected the ingredients and saw soy and biovat protein. The package promised strawberry flavour; Holly suspected the cereal had never been near a strawberry.

After her less than satisfactory meal, she wandered the narrow streets until she found herself at the market. She browsed the stalls aimlessly until the cold stares of stallholders who remembered her past behaviour became uncomfortable. The warehouse used by the shuttle crew loomed as she passed. She wondered how Jenkins, Commander Talbot, and the others were doing.

She returned to her room and spent money she could not afford to waste on a movie download, playing it on her memplant because she could afford nothing better. The movie killed a few hours, then the emptiness returned as it had before. Her small room held no answers.

＊

The maglev station had been designed with all the imagination of train stations since the dawn of the industrial age. The grey facade held a turnstile that allowed passengers through once the eye-level biometry scanner confirmed their identity. Jonah and his father followed the crowd of morning commuters through to the underground platform where silver cylinders floated on hidden superconductors.

They found places aboard the line to Washington DC and strapped in to the comfortable seats that Jonah's father had opted for when he booked the trip. Pages of the latest entertainment appeared when Jonah queried the on-board system; all free and available direct to his memplant or as a broadcast to the external devices older people preferred. He chose a new Kung Fu miniseries, Dragon Queens, as the train trundled out of the station and into an airlock. The doors sealed with the soft thump of airtight locks as the airlock pumped out the remaining air.

"Ladies and gentlemen, welcome aboard our Transcontinental service to Washington. For your own comfort and safety, please remain seated as we get underway."

The carriage rocked as it connected with the near-vacuum of the transit tube. The weight of extreme acceleration pushed them back into their chairs as the train ramped up to hypersonic speeds. Jonah managed to binge-watch three episodes before the train announced it was approaching their destination. Commuters rushed out of the maglev to join a queue for the autocars. They joined the line and before long were unpacking in a basic, but functional hotel room.

Jonah's father pulled a dark suit out of his brushed aluminium suitcase and handed it to Jonah. "I think this will fit."

Jonah gave the suit a sceptical glance.

"These people are the centre of power for our great country," said his father. "It pays to show a little respect.

Jonah grimaced, but changed into the suit.

His father straightened his tie. "We're lucky, I got us in to see one of the undersecretaries—Puckett, I think it is. When we get there, leave the talking to me." He paused to make sure Jonah was listening. "There's a language to government. If you don't speak it, they won't pay attention."

An autocar dropped them at an unmarked entrance that had no gate. The wall-mounted security system tracked their approach with range-finding laser and a large calibre barrel that followed a microsecond behind. The skin on the back of Jonah's neck crawled as he walked behind his father through the biometry scanners.

A service bot guided them through the building to a sitting room where Puckett was waiting. The undersecretary was a short, greying man with a worried frown etched across his forehead. "Please follow me and answer all questions that people may put to you."

Puckett led them down an extended marble corridor lined with the pictures of long-dead historical figures to a heavy oak door that gleamed with centuries of careful polish. Puckett held the door open and ushered them inside where the representatives of all seventy-three states of Panamerica sat waiting for them. There were fewer people than Jonah expected; only sixteen people sat in the chamber, the rest were telepresent as an avatar from their home state.

Puckett showed them to a roped off area on one side containing a row of seats and a speaker's podium with a microphone on a stand.

"Mr Barnes, could you please state your case for the record." Jonah could not see who spoke, but guessed it was the woman in the centre chair on the raised platform up in front.

His father paled but leaned toward the microphone. "Madame President, I believe we have an opportunity to restore Panamerica's helium-3 trade."

The room filled with a dead silence and the President gave an awkward cough. "I'm sorry, Mr Barnes, I meant your son. I want to hear from the young man who has spent time with these Moon Folk."

Jonah stood and took in the ranks of serious faces watching him. If his father could speak to these people, so could he. "I'm no one special. I just wanted to do the right thing." His words echoed from speakers hidden in strategic locations across the floor. "But, this isn't about me. Yesha, err, the Lady Yesha, First Empress of the Moon, does not wish for the suffering I have seen here; she only wants her people to be free. A strong trade in helium-3 would be the best thing for all of us. Madame President, I respectfully ask that you consider trading with the Free Moon."

He sat. There was nothing more to say.

One avatar in the serried ranks glowed amber.

"The Representative from Southern California has the floor."

"Fellow members, it has long rankled that we have had to pay our dues to Jingnan for every ounce of helium-3. Here's our chance to reboot with a brand-new paradigm. I say we run with this. If we speak to our friends in India,

I'm sure we can cut a deal on the transport that will provide synergies to both parties."

The room erupted in frenzied debate. Jonah sensed heavy traffic on his memplant and realised that spoken words were the smallest part of the discussion.

After almost an hour, the President held up her hand. "So that's a yes then." She stood. "By vote of the full Senate sixty-eight for and five against, The Federated States of Panamerica recognise Yesha Chen as first Empress of the Moon and request the development of regulated trade in energy and other goods. We further direct Jonah Barnes, in augment, to represent our interests in this negotiation."

After the proceedings had completed, Puckett took them back to the waiting room and offered them coffee.

Jonah was still in shock. "I'm not doing this. What makes them think I'll look after their interests?"

His father took in a sharp breath. "Of course, you'll do what is right for your country."

"Jonah has a fair question," said Puckett. "Do you know what 'in augment' means?" He took in their blank looks. "Jonah, you must accept a softmind augmentation. The softmind will guide your decision making."

"And if I don't accept it?"

"The President has issued this order under the state of emergency that has been in force since the helium-3 crisis started. Refusing the order will be considered treason and punishable by thought correction."

"Some choice." Jonah stared at the portrait of a dead hero on the wall. "Will I still be me afterwards?"

* * *

Holly twisted her bedsheets through a restless night until she couldn't take it anymore. After five days she had burned through the meagre supply of credit that basic income afforded. Two days stood between her and the next payment. She rose early and wandered the narrow street behind the market. Dark, worn-down buildings jostled with faceless warehouses and a half-empty autocar service lot. She stopped outside a faded blue door marked 'Zev' and rested one hand on the weathered brass doorknob. Behind the door, was her best chance to find the only work she knew she could do well. If she asked the right questions, she would find someone to help her make a nice little earner. It was this or go dull on basic. Looking once at the empty, grey street behind her, she took a sharp breath and opened the door.

The dim interior reeked of sweat and stale beer. Holly had only been in a bar once since she arrived in Maastricht; the Dutch frowned on underage drinking. She tried to act adult as she ordered a light wine from the autovendor. The wine came in a thick glass beaker. She took it to a corner table and sat.

It was not long before a tall guy with long blonde hair and a wispy moustache sat next to her. "Aren't you too young to be in here?"

"I can sit here if I want."

The guy looked her up and down. "You looking to buy?"

Holly gave a slight shrug. "Maybe I want to sell. I can lift."

The guy gave her a sly smile that did not extend to his eyes. "I can think of other work for a pretty, young thing like you. Pays better too."

"Eww! No."

The guy reached into his bag and pulled out a metallic circlet. "You ask me for work, but I don't know you. How can I trust you?" Rotating the slim circle between his thumb and forefinger, he held it out to her. "Put this on and I'll know where you are."

Holly seized the bangle and slammed it onto her wrist in one hurried motion like a hungry bird pecking at breadcrumbs. She gasped as the metal band tightened around her wrist, burrowed fine microfibres beneath her skin. Rearing back out of her seat, she knew rather than felt the nanites being pumped into her bloodstream. "What've you done to me?"

The smile slid from his face. "Sit, you don't want people remembering us."

She slid back onto her seat, her stomach quivering. "What do you want?"

The guy's smile did not return. "You know about slave bangles?"

Holly felt the blood drain from her face. "Get it off me!"

He shook his head. "Too late for that, it's already inside you. Can you feel the connections to your memplant? This one is special, I can send it a signal to override your impulse control. Let's say I give you a job to do and you cross me, I'll make it so you won't be able to help it; you'll want to do that job you just turned down."

"But, that's illegal."

"Like the work you're asking for is any better." He flicked his eyes to the entrance then back to her. "I know you from the market, I can use your skills. I need a police badge, not a fake—the real thing with the holoprint."

"Where am I going to get that?" she wailed.

"Not my problem. Bring it here next week and I'll give you a cut when I sell it." He gripped her wrist hard enough for Holly to feel the bones grate. "Don't mess up. You get the police interested in me and that bangle is all you'll know."

Holly pulled her arm free. "You'll get your badge." She beat a hasty path to the exit.

* * *

The pain woke him. Jonah groaned as he tried to sit up. A gentle hand on his shoulder restrained him.

"Lie still, Mr Barnes. The accelerated healing process is not instantaneous."

He opened his eyes to a blurred world, no one stood near him. "Who touched me?" His rough voice sounded loud in the quiet of the room.

"That was me. I am your care-bed and will be diligent in managing your recovery."

Jonah blinked, and the modern hospital room swam into sharper focus. "I'm thirsty."

A white-gloved hand held a disposable paper drinking straw to his mouth. Jonah was not surprised that the arm attached to the hand was jointed metal.

The door swung open and Dr. Martinez walked in. "The bed said you were awake. How are you feeling?"

Jonah's scrambled mind connected its scattered facts about Dr. Martinez. "My chest hurts. Is that where it is?"

"That is not surprising, I inserted two large organometal plates beneath your pectoral muscles. Think of it as having a manlier chest." He checked the screen at the foot of the bed. "This is a lot more complex than the injectable nanites that assemble a memplant in your head, you're carrying a whole softmind we hardwired to your brain. You may also experience minor discomfort from the optic fibre routed up the back of your neck."

"Will I know when it's working?"

The doctor adjusted a setting on the bed. "It will feel like a memplant to begin with, and as it learns more about your mental patterns, the softmind will open further."

Jonah spent the next three days in the recovery ward. The softmind remained silent apart from occasional visual flashes leaving fading grids of colour on his retina. The third night, a low droning kept him awake. Dr. Martinez said it was the softmind calibrating itself to his auditory nerve. On the fourth day it spoke.

"Memory eggplant reconnaissance."

Jonah started awake from a light doze. A new memplant icon flashed through his optic nerve. A roar of sound assaulted his auditory nerves as he activated the new app. He clapped his hands to his ears in a reflex that said his body did not understand his logical impulse that the sound was in his mind alone.

The sound broke off with a metallic click.

"Apologies," said a toneless voice, "Needed full internet access for updates. A language pack has been installed. Please access the green icon."

Jonah ignored the request, but a sudden overwhelming urge to do as it told him overrode his impulse control. He accessed the activation icon and gasped as the entire global network crammed into his head.

"Please hold while synaptic feedback is tuned."

The world receded to a manageable distance where the facts lurked beneath his conscious awareness. It was as if the collected knowledge of the world was in his memories and could be remembered with a thought. He shuddered, unable to decide if having so much power hidden within, elated or horrified him.

Dr. Martinez returned. "You have activation? Excellent. Now we can start the training."

Jonah moved out of the ward that afternoon and checked into a hotel near the hospital that the Senate officials insisted he use.

The hotel was a practical choice. He found a gym and exercised every morning. Dr. Martinez demanded his afternoons for hours of mental gymnastics.

The softmind had access to all the information it could use but had little to no ability to reason. Dr. Martinez started with simple deductive reasoning. "If the red is here, and the green ball is there, where is the blue ball?"

Jonah had to learn not to answer the question himself, but to remember the answer from the softmind. Dr. Martinez said it was like building a muscle, a lot of repetitions built ability, and with each ability came tougher problems. After a week, Jonah found himself attempting complex three-dimensional games, the kind of thing he had never been smart enough to play.

The next part gave Jonah nightmares. It started with a request from the softmind for access to his memories. Soon, he was moving memories into the softmind and giving it instructions to set up a submind. The submind used his own logic, almost as if a second, cold, emotionless Jonah sat alongside him solving problems.

The nightmares got worse when he tried to get the softmind to think about helium-3.

"Interdicted. You will negotiate a deal for Panamerica," blared the softmind. Jonah rapidly learned what was off limits.

After three weeks, the doctor declared the softmind ready. Dr. Martinez advised him to eat well every time he set up a submind; having two brains burning glucose was an enormous drain on the body's reserves. He gave Jonah a string of minor commands that would be useful and wished him good luck.

"Will I still be human, Doctor?"

The doctor smiled. "Your softmind is the finest we have ever implanted. You will be so much more than human."

Chapter 9

Intercession

The cold of solid basalt pushed through Yesha's thin robe and sank into her bones. She shifted to ease the discomfort. One day, she must commission a better throne. The sombre stone slab terrified her people with its austere majesty. It served as a perfect reminder of her uncle's rule, and everything she did not want to be.

Kaden stood below her, his shoulders drawn into a formal pose as he detailed progress on the new rail line to Beddau to the crowded audience. To Yesha, it sounded more like a litany of excuses for slow progress.

"Thank you, Kaden. That was most informative." She turned to Elizabeth. "What is our next item of business?"

"Doaran wishes to lay charges against two miners."

Jonah's former companion in battle stepped forward,

dragging two unwilling men behind her. "These two had fight in Cerata, old bar in Dome Seven. When I got there, they laying into people who tried stop them. Three others received minor medical treatment."

Yesha leaned forward and fixed the men with the glare she hoped displayed her anger. "Do you have anything to say for yourselves?"

The two men, unshaven and morose after an evening in one of the seediest bars in Chang'e, stared at their feet and said nothing.

"Very well. I find you guilty as charged."

A veil of silence descended on the crowd. Yesha caught herself as she rose to pronounce the sentence. The people expected her uncle's brand of discipline; a whipping followed by a stay in the cells. 'No,' she thought. 'We are a more enlightened people now.' She favoured the two men with a cold smile. "You will repay your debt to society. The macerator in the Beddau sewerage garden broke down yesterday. I sentence you to take the machine's place for a full lunar day of manual service."

The crowd groaned. Twenty-eight earth days in the stench-laden digesters that turned Beddau sewerage into usable compost taught a lesson that no one would forget. Doaran led the men off to the waiting guards, then came back and watched the rest of the court proceedings.

Elizabeth read out the next matter. "People of Dome Three complain of lice in dormitories." Yesha's court session dragged on through the minor complaints of the bored and the restless.

Once the sitting's formalities had been concluded, Doaran approached Yesha, and waited for a chance to speak. "Lady, fights becoming more common. I brought you two men today because they injured others, but I stopped many more. Fights not isolated incidents. Happened length and breadth of Mare Imbrium, from bars of Chang'e to canteens of New Karakorum. I even heard of fight in Beddau marketplace."

Yesha listened to this brave woman who had fought off armed attackers and charged into the face of death with no thought for her own safety. "I have a plan, but I need your help with it."

"Anything, Lady."

She beckoned Doaran closer. "This must stay between us for now. The droids will assist us."

Doaran's eyes opened wide.

Yesha shook her head. "We will speak no more of this now. Stay after the council meeting and I will explain." She rose and made for her chambers, hoping for a brief rest before the council meeting.

Her rest was all too brief. The council meeting in her chambers started with Amira complaining. "Jokarah produces tenth of what it could if we had more biocarbon. If only supply from Earth still came through."

Yesha tried to divert her. "How is Beddau producing right now?"

"Excellently, Lady. Too well, in fact. We harvested an overabundance of perskaw." Amira paused as if unsure, "We could trade perskaw with Earth; Jonah told me is no fruit like it up there."

"I'll think about it." Amira's request became the first of many. Not for the first time, Yesha hoped Jonah would tie up the deal with Panamerica soon. "Now, do we have any other business?"

"Not so much business, Lady, but tale I heard," said Elisabeth. "I met two men who travelled to abandoned mine of Lariah. After you said we would reopen Lariah, they went to see condition of mine. They found group of families living there, about two hundred people. Old administration gave permission to live as separatists, and eke out living in old mine. Our men told them about you and way things changed. Lariah people asked about moving to Chang'e or one of mines."

"As if we don't have enough mouths to feed," said Kaden. "This will add to our problems."

Doaran agreed. "If people join us, domes will get another two hundred people fighting and causing trouble."

Yesha suppressed her desire to tell the complainers to come back when they had useful answers. She held up her hands, and the room became quiet. "We will find a use for these people, anyone who survives the barren wastes of an abandoned mine will be strong and resourceful but let us not get too excited. Lariah is far and there is no easy way of getting here. Any people who come will arrive in small groups." She stood. "That is all our time for today. You may all leave, apart from you, Doaran. We have another matter to discuss."

Kaden gave her a sharp look at this pronouncement but stood and left with the others.

Doaran waited until Yesha invited her to sit.

"Is your exposure suit ready for an excursion?"

Doaran nodded.

"Then fetch it and meet me at the main airlock."

Yesha waited until Doaran left then checked an inventory she had checked before. Was it right to trust Doaran with this? Did she have a choice?

A short while later, she joined Doaran in the airlock. "We're going for a drive in my buggy."

Doaran grimaced but followed her out to the hydrogen buggy and climbed on board. Yesha gunned the accelerator and pointed the front towards Beddau.

After jolting across the grey plains for an hour, the gigantic Beddau airlock rose before them. Waiting beside the lock stood a battered mining truck, its massive tray filled to capacity with equipment. Doaran took in the line of bullet holes that stitched the side of the cabin. "Is this truck I drove during Suffering?"

"It was the only truck not on a register that I knew was still in working order."

Doaran raised her arms in the universal gesture for 'why?' used by people in exposure suits.

"I need you to drive it across Mare Imbrium to the Apennine Bench. Don't worry, I'll lead the way in my buggy."

The truck travelled much slower than the buggy. While Yesha threaded the buggy through the safest terrain she could find, Doaran lumbered behind in the oversized mining vehicle. The journey became one long arduous transit across dust littered with small boulders just big enough to stop a wheel. No sound travelled through the vacuum of the lunar atmosphere, but Yesha could imagine wheezing and rattling as the battered dump truck laboured up small hills.

The two women had not exchanged a word in hours by the time they entered the shadow of the Apennine Bench range. Toggling her suit's radio once to ensure Doaran listened, Yesha drove for a while further before stopping when she found what she had hoped for. Five gunmetal-grey droids materialised from the low dunes in a diamond formation. Doaran gasped. Yesha turned to check on her companion in the truck cabin. Doaran sat rigid, her stance obvious even through her exposure suit. "Benefactor, you brought supplies." The voice that came across the link did not even pretend to be human.

"I have everything you asked for: the tunnelling rig, two regolith extraction units, the heavy metals fractionator, and the sintering lens."

The five droids circled the truck. "Lidar scan confirms contents. You did not list the truck."

Yesha waved an arm at Doaran. "You'll need to join me on the buggy."

Doaran climbed down from the high cabin, then stood and stared across the gap to where the buggy waited. Her sharp, shallow breaths rattled across the communications link. She took in the droids to the left and right then sprinted across the gap.

"The truck is now yours."

"Acknowledged. Do you wish weapon designs transferred to your memplant?"

Yesha held up a slim black oblong. "Transfer it to this storage device." Her vision lost focus for a moment as she confirmed the transmission. She looked at Doaran as she started the buggy. "We should go home now, you a have a selection of new weapon designs to study."

Doaran's wide eyes appeared enormous through the glass visor of her helmet. "Why, Lady?"

Yesha hoped Doaran was ready for the answer. "Because I want you to build me an army."

* * *

Children swarmed the cobblestones outside the old-fashioned lolly shop. Happy mothers sat at outdoor tables enjoying more adult coffee and donuts, their child-minding duties taken by the cloud of mini-drones that hovered above the children. Holly spent a moment wondering how much the licence had cost the shop to sell that much sugar before she turned back to spy her target sitting at a corner table.

Sergeant Henrietta van Aalst, key member of the

Maastricht vice squad, avid coffee drinker, and mother of two sipped a latte, oblivious to Holly's scrutiny. After three days of careful observation, Holly knew everything she needed to know about the sergeant: How her target had an evening coffee after she collected her children from day-care, how she read the floating news display as she sipped her coffee, and how engrossed she would be in collecting her two small boys as soon as she finished.

The sergeant drained the last of her coffee as Holly positioned herself near the table, trying her best to be one more unobtrusive passer-by. She slipped in next to her target as the woman rose. The distraction of noisy children allowed Holly the moment she needed. She bumped up against the sergeant, one hand flicking to grasp the badge before anyone noticed.

A rock-solid hand grabbed Holly. "Stop! Thief!" The sergeant yanked on Holly's arm, bending the hand back and forcing the badge from her nerveless fingers. Holly pulled back hard, but the sergeant held tight.

The sergeant's eyes widened as she took in the bangle on Holly's wrist. "That's one of Pivetski's nasty gadgets."

Holly wriggled free and wasted no time bolting down the road.

"Wait!" yelled the sergeant. "I can help you."

Holly bolted around a corner, not waiting to see what she meant. The cops would arrest her. Pivetski or whatever his name was would activate the bangle. She had to get away and explain before the bangle turned her into a slobbering mass of self-induced sex hormones. Old grey houses turned to a meaningless blur as she pushed herself to get away.

Two blocks further, she ducked through a screening hedge to emerge in an alley she knew had no public safety cameras. She took a moment to catch her breath, listening intently for pursuing footfalls. None came. Above her, the white face of the moon shone in an indifferent sky.

Hours of careful sneaking along back alleys saw her emerge at her apartment. She curled into a tight ball on her small bed, unable to get comfortable. She should never have taken the gig. If she had stayed straight, none of this would have happened. Holly gripped a knuckle between her teeth. She should tip Pivetski that they had rumbled him, but the chances were good he would slave her, anyway. No, it was a safer bet to get out of Maastricht. Get far enough away that his signal wouldn't get to the bangle.

She surveyed the bland emptiness of her small room and knew where she could go. She grabbed the unopened bag of garam masala and headed for the marketplace.

Chapter 10

Distant Home

Jonah's room, back in Houston, was just as he had left it. Memories on the walls spoke to him as they had done before Washington; there hung the picture of Thomas, here the small scuff mark on the wall Jonah had left when he stumbled during a mock fight with Thomas; the past lay embedded in the everyday minutiae of life.

And yet, he took in so much more: the chemical composition of the paint on the walls; the shear stress of the bolts holding his bed together—an emotionless overlay that added deep information and analysis to the limits of his perception. Jonah looked at the chair beside his desk and knew how high he had to jump and how hard he must kick to destroy the chair. The martial artist inside him would have guessed, but now he knew the answers to the nearest microsecond and at a visceral level his muscles knew the exact percentage of effort to expend.

He wanted to call Yesha but stopped himself as he activated his memplant. Was it his desire or the Senate softmind's command to progress the deal? Did it matter? Jonah shrugged and placed the call.

She answered immediately. "I am so glad to hear your voice."

"It's time we negotiated a deal," said the softmind before he had a chance to speak.

"Jonah—" her voice carried clear across the quantum entanglement of the link. "Why are you speaking to me like that?"

"I'm sorry, that wasn't me." Empty silence stretched between them. Jonah tried for safer ground. "How is everyone at Chang'e?"

"Things are not going well. Come soon, I need you here, by my side." The memplant link expressed Yesha's longing through its limited range of emotional icons. "What's it like being back on Earth?"

"It's difficult." Jonah decided it would be safer to leave out the messier details of his time back in Houston.

"I'm so glad you went home. How are things with your father?"

Jonah tried to explain and failed. "Dad got me to Washington… They want to do a deal with you. They asked me to negotiate for them."

"That's wonderful, but how do you feel about working for the Panamericans?"

"I don't know. There are things that would be better if I explain them in person when I get there."

They ended the call, leaving Jonah alone in his room. Would she still want him with this thing lurking in his chest? Was it he who cared, or the softmind? The precise dimensions of the hallway outside his room occurred to him as he walked. He fought back a scream of frustration and went to find his father.

An hour later, Jonah and his father arrived at the edge of Deon Garcia Airfield where grey leviathans strained against the limpid blue of a summer sky. The autocar deposited them at the side of the airfield where a forest of ropes rose into the sky, restraining rank after rank of inflatable airships. They fought their way through the throngs of beggars to a counter where a harried official accepted Jonah's hand luggage for check-in.

The Senate had arranged for a first-class ticket all the way to India, and they assured him that a stratoliner would be waiting to take him into orbit.

Jonah was uncomfortable about going back to the country that deported him, but the softmind gave him no choice. A strong and unwavering impulse to get to India with all possible speed gripped him. He grasped his father's hand and said, "I guess this is goodbye then. Will you be okay on your own?"

His father clasped Jonah's hand in both of his as he looked Jonah in the eye. "I never thought I would say this, but I'm proud of you." He smiled. "Don't worry about me. You have an important job to do."

The airport announced the departure of Jonah's flight. Jonah put a hand on his father's shoulder, feeling the thin bones beneath. "Dad, there's so much we still need to say."

His father looked at the floor. "We'll have time to say it when you get back."

Jonah said goodbye and did not look back until the airship shuddered as the last ropes dropped to the ground. He found the thin figure of the old man within the sparse crowd and watched until clouds covered his view.

* * *

Holly stamped her feet against the side the crate, but no one came. Where were they? Her breath quickened in the enclosed space. No! She told herself. She had to do this. The further she got away from there, the better. She had been here before; there was no reason to panic like last time. Someone would be along to check on the noise.

The ration packs rustled beneath her. At least that was one thing she recognised. The plastic packs had been as soft as a pile of rubble when the shuttle put on its acceleration burn. She knew her back would be covered in bruises.

The Space Agency made it too easy to sneak aboard the shuttle; they should have learned after her last trip. Several months ago, Holly overheard two traders in the marketplace discussing how rats got in everywhere. Modern systems automated everything, but life had an annoying way of slipping through the cracks. There she was; another rat in the darkness. She stamped her feet again and received the same lack of response. If they were not going to rescue her, she had to do it herself. She kicked the end of the crate as hard as she could. The tough plastic gave a fraction.

The bracelet tingled. Holly held her breath, all thoughts of escape temporarily forgotten—Pivetski must have noticed her absence. The sensation that followed was nothing like desire, but more a primal need that she could no more deny than breathing. She had to find someone. She kicked again, wanting nothing more than to tear her clothes off and find one of the crew. Dim light rewarded her efforts; the hinge holding the lid was loose. She kicked again and this time the hinge popped apart. She crawled out into the darkened cargo bay and groped her way forward to the crew quarters. They were just as dark. "Where is everybody?" she asked, her voice plaintive with lack of sleep. Unbidden, her fingers began to unbutton her blouse.

"Holly?"

"Georgia? Where's the crew?"

"This is an automated supply run. I am flying solo. Why are you on my flight?"

"I wanted to go back." Holly tore her hands away from her chest and collapsed on a crash couch. "Help me!"

Georgia carried on without noticing, "It is a good thing you came to the crew cabin, protocol is to chill the cargo hold for better storage on auto runs."

"Please, Georgia."

"What's wrong?"

As Holly opened her mouth to speak, the horrible sensation of no longer having control of her own body began to fade. Outside the glass viewport, Earth was still visible as a sparkling orb in the distance. Holly traced the outline of Australia with one finger and imagined where Walker Creek would be. The aching emptiness of space filled the distance between the shuttle and the tall hoop pines of Walker Creek; enough space to be away from the activation signal. "Never mind; I made a mistake." The gentle hum of shipboard machinery filled the cabin. "I shouldn't have come, but I've got nowhere else to go." She drew a deep breath and considered her options. If she returned and confessed as soon as possible, the authorities would remove the bangle, when they fetched her from the stratoliner. Sure, the bangle would do horrible things to her and she'd earn punishment. On the other hand, if she made it to the Moon, Commander Talbot would just send her back. No easy answer presented itself to her.

Hours later, Holly prowled the empty ship. "Are you sure there's nothing to eat in here?" Holly searched the cabinets in the crew cabin without success. "I'm going to starve."

"That is unlikely. Our transit time is twenty-two hours," said Georgia.

She had a point, but Holly was already hungry. If only she had brought one of the disgusting ration packs up from the cargo deck.

"Now strap yourself in, I am about to start the deceleration burn. You can no longer go downstairs."

Holly did as it told her, just in time. The force of the burn crushed her into the padded seat. Blood drained away from her face. Georgia's voice came as though from a long tunnel. "I can't decide what you should do, but if you want to go back, stay hidden while we are docked. You can come out once I lift off and use the cabin until I dock with the stratoliner."

She clasped her fingers together so tightly that it hurt. What was she going to do? More community service was coming her way, if she went back, but was working for someone like Lintang so bad? The bangle itched on her wrist.

After a while, the pressure eased, and the shuttle settled onto the surface of the Moon with a thud. The dark walls of the base were visible through the viewport. Holly was stunned by how much it had grown.

Muffled clangs came from the cargo deck as moon-side crew unloaded heavy crates.

Holly shrunk back in her seat, still unsure of what she wanted.

Georgia's voice echoed through the cabin. "Seal integrity checked. Primary partition lock activated. Crew are free to board."

Holly held her breath. What was Georgia doing? The airlock between the cabin and cargo hold hissed open. Beyond the locker door, heavy boots clanged across the floor accompanied by the sliding rasp of helmet seals being undone. She leapt from her couch without thinking and dashed across to a tall storage locker. Stepping inside, she closed the door and tried to settle herself into the hard metal surfaces of the locker. Take off promised to hurt.

"I'm sure we left it in here last time." That was Jenkins.

"Try the storage cabinets," said a voice she did not recognise.

Holly froze. Cabinet doors banged around her. The full light of the crew cabin streamed into her locker.

"What the devil are you doing here?" A middle-aged man scowled down at her.

"I…"

"Oi, I know her." Jenkins' broad face appeared next to the scowl. "The commander will have kittens when he sees you."

Holly grinned at him. "Miss me much?"

Jenkins gave an exasperated sigh. "Come on, we'll get you sorted."

She gave him her best lost little waif smile. "Can't you just sneak me inside? I won't tell anyone."

"Sorry, love, protocol says the commander has executive authority. He'll have to say." He reached into the locker next to her and pulled out an exposure suit. "Better put this on. This shuttle needs to go."

Holly pulled the suit on and picked up the helmet. "Bye, Georgia."

"Goodbye, Holly.

She followed Jenkins out onto the grey dust. The new base loomed in front of them. "You built so much since I left."

"Not us," said Jenkins. "We've got ten q-fabs doing all the hard work for us."

The team had gathered the q-fabs in a ring, on the plain, some distance from the base where they were weaving a massive block structure from the dust.

"It's our new airlock," said Jenkins. "The techs say we can't get enough zinc from the mine; the ore is too poor. It means we can't build the dome, so the commander decided to expand the base."

Holly gaped as they rounded the corner of the base. It was at least twice as big as before.

"Still won't be big enough," said Jenkins. "Only two of us can control more than one bot. Most of us get a bad headache as soon as there's three running on our memplant."

A small dome was attached to the base by a thin walkway.

"That's our garden," said Jenkins. "No food yet, but right now it's collecting all our organic waste." He grinned. "That's the botanist's nice phrase for the sewerage."

The same plastic tube she had walked through before still served as the airlock. Holly stepped through with the other two and removed her suit. The passageway echoed with voices from further along. The base sounded full and busy, so different from when she was last here.

"How many crew do you have?" she asked Jenkins.

"Sixty-two. Would have been a lot more if we could have got the dome started." He knocked on a plain aluminium door as the floor rumbled with the shuttle's departure. "Sir, we've got an unexpected visitor."

* * *

The crescent moon shone above them in the burnt umber of an Indian twilight as the airship made fast in the Hyderabad airfield. Jonah handed back his half-empty glass of Californian sparkling wine and looked at the slim white crescent in the sky, so tantalising in its closeness.

He stepped on board the transfer bus, delighted to encounter air-conditioning. Jonah sat, luxuriating in the flow of cool air and steeling himself for the dimly lit crowds of the arrivals hall.

The crowds did not disappoint him; the reek of over-packed humanity washed over him as he walked inside. Rows of patient people waited for their turn at a customs window. How quickly the world had learned to wait once the energy wasted on auto-check-in was no longer available. Standing in the queue, he shuffled forward until the cold of a snub-nosed pistol in the small of his back stopped him. He turned to see the same soldier who arrested him before.

"Come quietly and I won't be forced to shoot you."

Jonah was steered toward the unmarked door they had used last time. Inside, they marched to the same holding cell. Two junior soldiers sat him in a chair and bound his arms and legs. They left, and Jonah sat, wondering what would follow. Once again, he was powerless. No, that was not true. His lips curled in a faint smile as he set up a submind.

The soldier returned. "Why are you back in India, Mr Barnes?"

Jonah gave him his undivided attention as the submind finished its task. "I'm going back to the Moon," he said, then laughed as the submind produced the answer he hoped for. "I know why you sent me to Panamerica, Major Ravindra Patel."

The man rocked as though Jonah had slapped him. "How do you know my name?"

"You don't want to know the answer to that."

Major Patel drew his pistol and held it in front of Jonah's face. "You and I will go for a ride." He freed Jonah's legs and walked him out of the cell. Jonah's shoulders tensed as the major stepped in behind him. The softmind calculated the angle of a spinning back kick with the highest probability of receiving a minimal gunshot wound. Jonah forced himself to calm down; the major was still his best way off Earth.

They made their way through the building, past the incurious eyes of other security staff. If the major wished to take a prisoner for interrogation, it was none of their business. Doors opened, and gates were unlocked until they stood beside a battered four-wheel-drive vehicle old enough to still have a steering wheel. "Get in." The major bound his hands to a post on the passenger side long since scarred by other captives.

As the ancient electric motor rattled into life beneath the bonnet, the major took the wheel and drove. The sprawling mass of Hyderabad fell behind them, and the road narrowed from eight lanes to two as the transport climbed toward verdant hills. Jonah followed their journey using a map in his memplant. He instructed the softmind to assess possible destinations, but the results were inconclusive.

After an hour, the major pulled over at a roadside stall and returned with two disposable paper cups. He inserted a bamboo drinking straw in one and wedged it in position so that Jonah could reach it. "It is chai, drink or you will dehydrate in this heat."

Jonah sucked on the straw and coughed. The chai was a sweet tea spiced with hints of exotic spice.

Major Patel laughed. "It won't kill you."

Jonah drew on it, grateful for the liquid and sugar. Using a submind for so long had drained his blood-sugar levels and left him tired and listless. Below his conscious thought, the softmind accessed his memplant's GPS locations, and arrived at a conclusion. "Why are we heading to a memplant black spot, Major?"

Patel turned his eyes from the road to fix Jonah with a firm stare. "You will not speak of that again."

After they had travelled for an hour, in which the major did not say another word, they turned off onto a track that was little more than two furrows in the red earth. The transport bumped and rattled over the road as they arrived at an entrance marked only by a hand-carved wooden board proclaiming, "Tiger Sanctuary."

Narrow ruts carried them deeper into the jungle until the major stopped at a rise overlooking a patch of open grassland. The rustling whirr of small insects surrounded them.

"I will free your hands now. Please don't run away. This is the Srisailam tiger reserve. There is a chance you would make it out before the tigers found you, but I would rather you do not risk it.

"I wanted to talk to you before you left, but there are too many ears in Hyderabad and too many watcher bots on the memplant networks. This way we can speak."

Jonah nodded, unsure of what to say next. The softmind churned through a storm of tactical information.

The major stared out at the empty landscape for a long moment before he waved a hand to take in the sweep of grassland before them. "This is the largest tiger reserve in India. Over two hundred of the deadliest predators on the continent live here now, but they only survive because people made it so.

"I don't know how you know I am an agent of the Panamerican Senate, and it does not matter, but I beg you not to tell anyone of this. We all do what we must to survive."

Jonah took a sip of the chai, inhaling clove and cardamom.

"If Panamerica forms a trade deal with the Moon, India will provide as much support as it can in return for a fair share of helium-3."

"I'll discuss it with the Lady."

"Thank you." The major opened his mouth to say something else, but then his eyes widened. He pointed out onto the edge of the grass where a lithe shape wove through the long grass.

Jonah held his breath as the tiger looked their way, inspecting them as if they might be prey. Unsatisfied with its prospects, it disappeared into the bush.

The major held up the carbon fibre ties that had bound Jonah and gave an apologetic laugh. "We will have to resume this charade until I deport you back to the Moon."

Jonah spent the return journey thinking. If Panamerica took advantage of the Indian spaceport, they could transport enough helium-3 to power the world.

* * *

The administrator's suite was too big for Yesha. Before the Suffering, she had occupied the two rooms along the east end while Uncle had used the entire suite for his affairs. Now it was hers. The main office held pools of light and shade that were meant to complement a serene stillness. Instead it felt abandoned, almost haunted by people long since gone.

Yesha sat at the desk with its empty expanse of dark Earth wood and reached a hand out to the sealed glass globe with its collection of slow-moving shrimp and dark moss. The sealed ecosystem signified the challenge of running this colony. If only Uncle had understood the lessons.

Chang'e and its mines were not closed samples of Earth, but an independent state open to any ship that came from Earth. Ships that came and brought people and their ideas and sometimes their diseases. The ships were coming; whatever the deal the Panamericans offered, many more ships would come.

Beyond the wide window, the blue marble of Earth hung in the sky. Jonah was still there. She missed his solid presence in the way rivers needed rain. He was on his way, but Earth had changed him. He had been so strange in their last call, as though another Jonah, more focused on Earth spoke to her.

Her memplant flashed a green bulb icon through her visual cortex. A text message from Elizabeth followed. "Doaran and team ready for you, Lady."

She stood and dragged herself over to her cavernous walk-in wardrobe. The smart mirror lit as she entered, showing her a tired Moon Folk woman who looked too thin. Her simple moonsilk robe was wrong for this. She scanned the racks of clothing and selected a dark suit with a military appearance. The mirror showed her wearing the suit. Satisfied with the message her outfit was sending, she went in search of Doaran.

Doaran's assembled troops stood to attention in neat ranks when she arrived. Three hundred grey-clad fighters in rows of ten filled the dust plain in front of Yesha's throne. Yesha gave a brief nod towards Doaran. "You have been busy. I am impressed."

"Was easier than expected. Most are fighters from the Suffering and happy to serve." She gave Yesha a feral smile. "Better weapons this time."

Kaden had driven the massive industrial workshops of New Karkorum to produce a collection of exotic weapons from the plans provided by the droids. She saw neural disruptor darts that could stop an approaching enemy's muscles; an electromagnetic pulse canon that fried electronics; and the dark tubes that the droids described as lattice traps.

"Fist of Chang'e, present arms." Doaran's voice thundered across the floor.

Three hundred weapons rose as one.

"First Finger, prepare to fire."

The row to her left turned and aimed the tubes of their lattice traps toward a line of dark basalt monoliths set up for the occasion.

"Fire!"

The solid mass of monoliths shivered and became insubstantial then slumped to the floor in untidy piles of dust.

Yesha stood with her mouth open.

"We don't know how it works, but it destroys any solid as far as we can tell," said Doaran. "Kaden thinks it disrupts molecular bonds."

Kaden appeared from among the councillors behind her. "Now we will be able to control the difficult people. Soon we'll have order and stability again."

Yesha ignored Kaden's glee and assumed her most regal pose. She did not want to be her uncle, but this was a time for strength. "Well done, my people." Now she had a tool to bring fear to those who opposed her. Kaden thought this was a police force, but she had other goals in mind. Let the collected nations of Earth come if they dared. The Moon would be ready.

Chapter 11

Reunion

A voice intruded, rousing Yesha from her restless sleep. She rose and wrapped herself in a silk robe. "What is it, Elizabeth? It is past the middle of the sleep cycle."

"Indian shuttle has landed."

Yesha shook the fatigue from her head. "Wake Doaran. Tell her to meet me at the main airlock with a full complement of the Fist of Chang'e." She paused a moment. "And, have them armed."

Yesha took her time dressing. The Indian representative could wait outside the airlock until the troops were in place. She chose the black robe with its silver trim and after a moment's thought, the platinum tiara she seldom wore. Meeting with her people was one thing, meeting a foreign power another.

When she arrived at the airlock, Doaran's troops lined each side with the dark tubes of their lattice traps aimed at the lock. The troop layout was at once practical and awe-inspiring. As the Indian representatives came through the airlock, they would first see the armed might of the Fist of Chang'e deployed across the vast entry hall then the spectacular tier of buildings that dominated the view in Dome One—the full wealth and power of an independent Moon. She frowned. "Get those lattice traps down," she told Doaran. "It will be catastrophic if you disintegrate the lock."

"Safe enough, Lady. We found way to scale down range."

Yesha took a deep breath. She hoped Doaran was right. A small part of her wondered what a lattice trap would do to human flesh and decided she did not want to know.

A single figure in an exposure suit stood outside the lock.

"Show our guest in," she said.

The hiss of air accompanied the grinding roar of the lock cycling. The person stepped through and raised their hands when they saw the barrels. They reached carefully for their helmet latch and removed it.

"Jonah," yelled Doaran, and ran over to greet him. The guards, seeing her reaction, lowered their weapons.

Yesha kept her distance, stilling the impulse she had to run over and throw her arms around Jonah. "The people of the Moon welcome you, Mr Barnes. In what capacity do you come before us?"

Doaran stepped back and tried to look formal. She cast a sheepish grin toward Yesha.

Jonah squared his shoulders. "I come as an emissary of Panamerica, here to negotiate the supply of helium-3 for our great nation."

"Welcome, honoured guest. Join me in my chambers and

we will discuss these matters," said Yesha. She also sent his memplant a private message, 'I am so glad to see you.'

'Let us discuss the trade deal,' came the instant reply.

She turned to look at him and raised her eyebrows. His face remained blank.

'What's going on? Did the trip upset you?'

'I am well. Let us talk about the trade.'

She left it at that and led the procession to her chambers. Doaran and the guards peeled off as they walked until only the two of them and Elizabeth remained. Yesha nodded at her and Elizabeth turned off to her small adjoining suite.

The door closed behind them. Yesha's stomach trembled as she took off her tiara and shook her hair out. Rushing over to Jonah, she quickly kissed him and pressed her body into his, comforted by his physical presence. Resting her head against his chest, she suddenly pulled away, startled. 'What's that inside you?'

Jonah took a deep shuddering breath. "I'm sorry. I wanted to tell you, but it wouldn't let me." He stepped away from her and slumped on the reclining bench that occupied one wall.

Yesha wanted to rush to him, but her black robe reminded her of who she was. She took one step further back. "What have you done?

"It was the deal. The Senate wouldn't trust me, so they sent this thing with me. Most of the time it's mine, but a small part compels me to trade on their behalf."

Yesha crossed her arms as she turned away from him, trying to contain the hollow pain that followed his words. She kept her voice low, as she said what she must, "I can't have you near me until we solve this. I'll get Elizabeth to set up guest quarters for you."

"Please…" Jonah's voice held a note of pleading she had not heard before. "Can't we be together for a while before all of this starts?"

She shook her head without looking at him, unsure of what she would do if she turned around. Behind her Jonah's footsteps faded towards the door.

***

The flimsy aluminium door swung open and Commander Talbot's face turned from polite concern to instant anger when he saw who was standing behind it. "I thought I sent you back to Earth." He looked at Jenkins. "Get that shuttle to abort its launch. I want her out of here."

"Too late, sir. The shuttle did a quick turnaround."

Talbot glared at her. "We really do need to build a brig. What am I going to do with you?"

"I'm sorry, Commander." Holly clutched her hands together. "I know this was a big mistake. I'll try to stay out of your way."

"Yes, you damn well will. I want you back on the next shuttle."

"You don't have to be rude."

Talbot pointed out the wide window to where the mountain ring surrounding Plato Crater loomed. "Behind those hills lies Chang'e, a country that may be planning to send battle droids against us for all I know. My team doesn't need another distraction."

"I won't be a bother."

The commander clenched his fists on the desk in front of him. "You stupid girl. This is not a holiday camp you can breeze in and out of as you please."

Holly cursed the hot tears she felt coming. "Didn't you ever make a mistake? I did something dumb." She showed him the bracelet and explained what she had done. "I was hungry and bored, and now I'll pay for it. You don't even know what this thing does to me. I'll keep out of the way, I swear."

The commander's gaze softened. "Everyone makes

mistakes sometimes. The next shuttle is due in two days. Go and help in the kitchen and try to stay out of trouble."

Holly followed Jenkins out as fast as she could, trying her best not to cry.

Jenkins led her to the room they had dubbed the kitchen. Inside, aluminium racks along one wall held rows of foil ration pouches. A lingering cardboard odour of ration packs spiced by the faint cordite scent of moon dust permeated the kitchen. Holly had a sudden intense longing for the rich spices of Lintang's kitchen.

Two men worked at a long metal bench that occupied the middle of the kitchen, pouring the contents of ration packs onto dull metal plates. At least the crew no longer ate out of pouches. She settled in next to the other two and prepared the last of twenty meals. She learnt that the crew ate in shifts and took it in turns to prepare meals and wash up afterwards. The scullery contained a stainless steel box set under a spigot that served boiling water direct from the heat sink.

After the meal, Jenkins found her contemplating the spigot when he came to show her to her room.

"The plates are nice," she said.

"Made them myself. I fed two q-fabs the raw materials and downloaded a design from an Earth site."

Holly walked on beside him, enjoying having eaten her first full meal in days. She stopped. "Could you make a pot?"

"Don't see why not. How big?"

She held out her hands. "If you can make me a pot and a spatula before the next shift, I'll try to improve your dinner."

Jenkins stopped at the door to the room which the commander had assigned to her. She said goodnight and closed the door. It was a different room to last time only because it was further down the corridor. The same narrow window illuminated another uncomfortable crash couch mattress.

The next day, her muscles ached from the hard bed. She got up and stretched, then noticed how grubby she had become after the long day and her hard work in the kitchen. She wandered off in search of Jenkins.

"Where can I wash?" She blushed. "I could use a bath after yesterday."

"Come on, I'll show you," he said and led her to the garden dome end. He opened the last door before the dome airlock. A durable woven plastic sheet printed in bright florals partitioned the narrow room. "Welcome to our luxury bathroom." He reached behind the plastic curtain and grabbed a cheap q-fab printed bucket. "Fill this from the spigot in the kitchen. There's a drain in the floor, toss the rest of the water in when you're done."

Later and much cleaner, she was back in the kitchen where she found a brand-new pot and a stainless steel bar that acted as a spatula. The pot was a snug fit for the scullery box. She put it down inside and selected twenty ration packs labelled creamy chicken.

The contents of twenty packs filled the pot to the brim. Holly ran hot water from the spigot into the box surrounding the pot until the pot almost submerged. She stirred the contents with her makeshift spatula as heat from the water infused the chicken. The aroma of golden chicken filled the kitchen.

Holly straightened to ease the cramp she got from squatting next to the pot. Her hand brushed the lump in her pocket. She pulled out the packet of garam masala that Lintang had given her. Hints of exotic spice wafted from the package. She wondered how Lintang would have used it, then shrugged and threw in a respectable pinch. The aroma of the kitchen started to remind her of the Blauw Zwaluw. She refreshed the water to get more heat into the pot.

A crew member she did not recognise strolled past the kitchen and stopped. "What's that? Doesn't smell like the usual junk."

Holly smiled. "Help me get it dished up and we can take it to the mess hall."

It was not long before she set twenty plates of steaming chicken curry on the table in front of a hungry squad.

Commander Talbot came in with the rest of the crew and sat down to a chorus of appreciative voices praising the hot food that didn't taste as if it came out of a packet.

Talbot gave her a considered look as he ate.

After the shift had eaten, Holly carried the stack of dirty plates back to the kitchen and got to work washing them. She heard a low cough and turned to find Talbot standing at the door to the kitchen. "You have hidden talents, young lady."

"I know a little. I learnt from a great cook in Maastricht."

The commander came into the kitchen and stood across the bench from her. "The agency decided we should have a balanced diet supplied as easy-to-store ration packs. In true military fashion, nobody thought about how dull it would be to eat the same seven packages week after week." He stood, looking at the pot she had used. "I saw more smiles today than I have in weeks. My team is full of soldiers and engineers; none of them can cook like you just did. If I clear it with Central Command, would you be interested in cooking for us?"

Holly froze for a moment, not believing what she heard, then squealed in excitement and threw her arms around the commander. "Yes, thank you. I'll cook the best food you've ever had."

The commander gently disentangled himself from her. "Go to the old shuttle and chat to Benny. I'm sure it can do something about that ridiculous bracelet."

"Thank you, Commander." Holly realised she was gushing. "But I'm safe as long as I'm here."

He gave her an indulgent smile. "Get it fixed anyway. You are still going back on the next shuttle."

Holly's lip trembled, "I thought you said I could stay. They'll get me if I go back now."

Giving her a good-natured scowl, the commander pushed her out the door as he said, "At least my troops listen when I tell them to do something. You need to go back to buy food for us. Don't worry, I'll send Jenkins along to look after you. Now, move it!"

Benny wasted no time in connecting to the bangle once Holly had suited up and dashed across to the shuttle. "Such poor-quality coding, it's criminal. Fancy using sub-optimized recursion. Lie down, Holly. You may feel a little faint."

Most of the crash couches had been stripped and repurposed as bedding for personnel at the base. Holly made it to the last remaining couch moments before the worst dizziness she had ever felt slammed into her. "Ugh! That's horrible."

"Hold on, almost there," said Benny, sounding far too reasonable.

Another tidal wave of nausea flooded through her before the bracelet opened with a tiny click. Holly ripped it from her arm and flung it across the cabin as hard as she could in her weakened state.

"There. All done," said Benny. "My medical files say the nanites will flush out in a day or two as long as you drink lots of water."

Holly staggered to her feet and stood, holding the

edge of the couch for support. "Thank you, Benny. I don't know what I would have done." She wobbled over to her helmet and sealed it back in place. "See you later. I've got a meal to go and cook."

* * *

Yesha knocked on the door to the suite reserved for guests of state. It was a timid knock, one that asked for permission to enter, not the imperious request of the ruler of the Moon's people. Jonah opened it then walked back in without saying a word. She followed, tracing the line of his shoulders as he walked. Inside, a faint odour of dust and rooms unused since her uncle's time met her.

Jonah sat in the formal lounge and looked at her to see if she would join him. She chose the seat across from him. "How are you feeling?" She castigated herself for the inane comment, but she had to start somewhere.

He smiled and shrugged. "I've had a good sleep."

"Jonah…" she drew a deep breath. "Will you let me talk to the other?"

"What do you mean?" he asked. She could not tell if it was him or the machine that spoke.

"I want to form a direct mind to softmind connection." Her eyes hardened. "Look in Jonah's memories. You will see how I spoke to the droids."

Jonah's eyes lost focus. "Connection will be permitted for the purposes of sale treaty negotiation only."

Yesha permitted herself a small smile. She lay back on the couch, closed her eyes and began a cycle of deep breathing. The suite receded as her consciousness sank inside herself, stilling her mind for what was to follow. Her senses became aware of her body, of its weight upon the couch. She embraced the sensation and allowed it to grow beyond her until her perception embraced the room and the cold logic that watched her mind from where Jonah lay. She reached for it, and a connection bloomed in her awareness.

'How is your connection possible? My memory banks do not contain a record of human to softmind linkage at Alpha level.'

'And yet, here I am. What is it you want?' Yesha asked while she pushed deeper into the core of the softmind. A secure firewall blocked her.

'Panamerica seeks to have a trading arrangement equal to that of other nations.'

'What does Panamerica offer in return for helium-3?'

She pushed further while the softmind prepared its answer, skirting the blocked section. Connections to Jonah's memories and feelings appeared. She moved down an array of his innermost feelings too private to bear, and drew back, ashamed of having been so close without an invitation.

'We offer a line of credit in a bank of your choosing.'

'Completely unacceptable. What control does the Moon have over an Earth-side bank?'

The softmind computed. She forced herself to go deeper into Jonah's feelings, hoping he would find it in himself to forgive what she was about to do.

Feelings became intentions which became actions. The softmind's tendrils spread throughout Jonah's mind.

'We propose the establishment of an independent bank.'

'Bring me the terms and we can discuss it.'

She found the dense fibre that enveloped Jonah's will.

'Release him,' she said. *'I can see how you control Jonah's compulsion.'*

'Access denied.'

Yesha realised administrative access lay hidden deep behind the firewall. She could break it, but would Jonah still be Jonah if she did so? She cut the connection and brought herself back to reality. Glimpses of Jonah's memories and feelings lay inside her like the rainbow sheen of oil on water. She experienced the pain of his past, the triumph of his victory during the Suffering, and knew the depth of his feelings for her.

Jonah's eyes struggled open as if from a deep sleep. She went to him and put her hands on his shoulder. "Please forgive me," she said, and ran from the room unable to bear it a moment longer.

Elizabeth waited in the corridor. "Lady, council waits for you."

Yesha wanted to snap at the stupid woman, to tell her to go away so she could be alone in her misery. Instead, she took a deep breath and followed Elizabeth, composing herself as she walked.

The council were in full cry when she arrived. Kaden stood at the far end of the table holding forth. "We should send the Panamerican home. We don't need the deal. I hear from contacts that Jingnan has lines of supply from the time before the troubles. They can buy our helium-3 and on-sell it to everyone, just as they used to do."

"And then?" Yesha took her place at the head of the table. "Do we become Jingnan's lackey? Happy to accept whatever they offer us."

"That is such an immature view. We need a strong trading partner, and I think we need to show more respect."

"What does that mean?"

"Disband the show of force we see you building."

The council turned as one to stare at him then turned to see how Yesha would respond.

Yesha's stomach tightened. How dare he speak to her like that? She kept her face impassive as she spoke and showed no one the tumult raging inside her. "It is not for you, Kaden Bachmann, to decide what is best. I will not tolerate the interference of Earth nations in the affairs of my people. The deal with Panamerica will go ahead."

Kaden had the good grace to take a seat and not respond. Yesha hoped she had terrified him.

"I am negotiating the terms of the trade treaty with the Panamerican representative. We will bargain for a line of credit usable with all Earth vendors. Our helium-3 will buy technology, luxury goods, and more tons of biocarbon than we can use. The people will grow rich off this deal."

A scattered cheer rang around the table.

Yesha rose and made for the exit, hoping that no one saw how she shook.

Chapter 12

Strategic Acquisition

Lintang raised her glass and took an appreciative sniff. "A grüner veltliner, I think, but not one from Europe." Muted conversation and the quiet clink of cutlery filled the Blauw Zwaluw on a lazy Sunday afternoon.

"How did you know?" asked Holly, her eyes wide. "It's Australian, I found it in an autovendor down the road." She flicked her eyes to where Jenkins sat alongside her in the narrow booth enjoying a Dutch pilsner. She didn't want him mentioning just how far along the road the only autovendor stocked with Australian wine had been.

"I have had a lifetime of pairing food and wine. This will go well with dishes like nasi lemak and Gado Gado; the aromatics complement our spice selection." Lintang took a small sip and placed the wine in a ray of sunshine which highlighted the pale golden liquid. "But, you are not here to trade tasting notes."

Holly swallowed, she hoped Lintang would help. "I never told you why the police arrested me, and you were kind enough not to ask." She took a deep breath of spice-laden air. "I went to the Moon."

Lintang's face was a map of well-hidden disbelief.

"It's true. I ended up going by accident." She told Lintang the entire story ending with Talbot's offer. "And, now I don't know what to do. He trusted me with this and I don't want to disappoint him. Can you help me?"

Lintang stood. "Come," she said, heading toward the kitchen. She went to a wall where rows of spices stood in an antique wooden cabinet. The ghosts of faded names on each drawer were printed in a black so pale the wood shone through. Lintang ran a hand over the porcelain drawer knobs: cinnamon, ginger, star anise; she stopped at cassia and pulled it open to show the slivers of bark inside. "Rijsttafel has been a part of Dutch culture since the first ships sailed back from the East Indies carrying their chests of dried spices. In my old country, we used the fresh spices, but those plants don't grow in the cold. Here, cooks had to use spices dried to survive the long journey from the tropics." She waited for Holly to take in what she was saying.

Holly frowned at the spice rack for a moment then hugged Lintang. "Thank you so much. I must go shopping."

"Before you do that," said Lintang. "Come back tomorrow. I will send you to a friend; you need to see how a modern restaurant works."

Holly spent the night in her small hotel room. Jenkins had grumbled when she found the cheapest rooms she could; a pair of windowless cabinets buried deep within a shopping mall. The commander had given her a slim line of credit for the trip, but she wanted to save as much money for supplies as possible. The hotel was as safe as it was cheap; there was almost no chance of the wrong people seeing her on this side of town. Besides, she felt as safe as she could be with the big marine accompanying her every move. Her wrist still itched when she thought about the horrible bracelet.

The next day, Lintang took them to Auberge Herfe, a brightly lit neo-roman restaurant overlooking the river. The kitchen looked more like the flight deck of the shuttle with its two serverbots chopping vegetables much neater than she ever could. She learnt about using constant temperature sous-vide baths to cook meats and how vacuum fryers allowed the chef to cook at low temperatures. As important were the fresh vegetables the restaurant bought from the markets; vegetables grown by local farmers and transported the shortest distance possible.

The flood of new ideas sparked a hungry curiosity deep inside her. Catching herself staring at a vacuum flavour extraction unit, she thought, 'I could use that'. Cooking was something Mum did in the kitchen, but today Holly saw an open door to a life she had never dreamed she could have. Holly left Auberge Herfe with a whirlwind of designs rushing through her head. She couldn't wait to get back to the Moon to try out her new ideas for how to use the hot water from the heat sink to make a sous-vide bath. If only there was a way to get fresh vegetables. She used her memplant to take pictures and make notes of everything, then sent it to her Moon data store as a long rambling post.

The two weeks until the flight passed in a blur. Every day, Jenkins delivered her to mandatory safety briefings where the world's dullest softmind rambled on about the terrifying consequences of sudden decompression on a world without an atmosphere. The dry lectures gave Holly nightmares once she understood how close she had come to dying in her previous adventures.

The space agency allowed her two crates to pack as she wished with specific requirements; two crates, no more, no less, not to exceed the specified weight. It was two crates they could not use for something else. The market became the hardest part of her day as she haggled with vendors who no longer saw straight through her now she had credit to spare. She loaded up on spices and dry goods like rice, tough enough to survive the journey. A butcher prepared a selection of meats for her in a cryovac bag and told her the meat was good for up to two weeks without refrigeration.

Holly limited herself to one indulgence, a carbon steel chef's knife with an antique woodgrain finish. She thought it was the most beautiful thing she had ever owned.

Too soon, the time had evaporated. She checked the packing on the crates that now occupied a shelf in the same warehouse one last time before joining the new crew at the airport.

Going through customs as an official traveller was a novelty after her previous unauthorised trips. The crew were friendly, but distant. They had spent weeks training together. She and Jenkins followed them as they boarded the stratoliner and found their seats. Once she strapped herself in, Holly lay back as they took off and dreamed of recipes she could try.

* * *

"Kia!" the battle cry erupted from a hundred throats as fists slammed into the metallo-plastic poles in front of them.

"Again," said Doaran. "I want to hear the poles rattle from your strike."

The clatter of fists against plastic resounded through the emptiness of the vast cavern that housed the New Karakorum receiving bay. The fighters made a long grey line under a string of harsh floodlights. Beyond their shallow pool of light, darkness swallowed everything.

Jonah stood to one side and observed the practice. Yesha had limited his access to many areas, but Doaran's training ground was as neutral a place as any while things were difficult. It wasn't fair that they couldn't be together while this thing in his chest lay between them. Putting thoughts of Yesha from his mind, he focused on Doaran who prowled in front of the fighters like a ravenous beast. Gone was the wild woman who had fought alongside him. Now, Jonah saw a lithe and deadly frame filled with the confidence that could only be won by killing.

She saw him and waved. "You coming to train with us?"

"I might be," said Jonah as he walked to where she stood.

She cast a critical eye over him. "You look bigger. What have you done to chest?"

"Let's call it a hidden muscle," he said. "What have you been teaching these guys?"

"Some basics. We focus on weapons instead." She snapped her fingers. "Cutter, take over. Dov, Marya, come with me." She motioned for Jonah to follow.

"You been back to Beddau?"

Jonah shook his head. "I want to, but there hasn't been time yet. Has it changed?"

Doaran grinned. "More than you imagine. Many people

live there now. Gardens produce food for half of Mare Imbrium." She gave his shoulder an uncharacteristically gentle touch. "She would want to see you."

Before Jonah had a chance to respond, Doaran stopped next to a pile of black metal pipes. "You saw when you arrived. Now you see what they do. Dov, Marya, take out rocks."

Dov and Marya turned two of the tubes towards the heap of boulder-strewn rubble. The tubes hissed, and the rubble became a pile of slag.

"Whoa! What are they?"

"New tech from droids. Got other stuff also.

"Neuralisers, electronic killers, and one more thing you going to love." She waved a small baton controller and lights further in the darkness flooded a second patch of floor.

The thing they illuminated reminded Jonah of a grasshopper if a grasshopper twice his height and constructed of dull grey metal existed.

"Earth people laugh, but we call it hopper. Good for surface travel and climbs hills faster than buggies."

"That's amazing," said Jonah. "How do you control it?"

"Come," said Doaran, waving at all three, "Seats six. Won't need suits if we walk around the receiving bay."

Jonah didn't need to be invited twice. He followed Doaran as she scrambled up ladder spines that protruded from a leg and found three rows of two open bucket seats along the back. He took one of the two front seats, allowing Doaran to take the driver's seat. Once the other two had strapped in, she placed her hands on two short joysticks and the hopper moved forward.

"Easiest thing to drive," she said. "Small softmind manages balance and all I do is point. Runs fast too. Can't show you in here; not enough room."

Jonah thanked her as he got off and left her to her training. The advanced weaponry and large military presence suggested Yesha had plans. He thought about the strategic impact of an armed Moon force then wondered whether he or the softmind expressed concern. He decided not to examine that thought.

***

The new kitchen was amazing. To be honest, it was the old kitchen with a brand-new cooking range. Holly had launched herself at Jenkins squealing with excitement when he led her into the compact cooking space. The big softy had maintained a perfect stiff upper lip while he secretly sent notes of everything Holly looked at to the engineering team at Plato Crater. The clever engineers ran pipes of scalding water straight from the heat sump into a sous-vide bath. Holly could set the precise temperature using a simple tap that controlled the speed of flow. She looked forward to testing it on the side of beef she had packed. They had also provided an induction cook-top with strict instructions only to use it during daylight hours when the solar array produced enough energy. Right now, full darkness showed through the one slit window into the kitchen. The new gadget would have to wait.

As she unpacked her new provisions into a neat set of aluminium shelves, two of the team were tinkering with a large corner cabinet they said was her new refrigeration box. Holly did not understand how a stream of hot water could make something cold, but the engineers assured her it was possible.

"Can you use these?" Holly turned to find Nathan the horticulturist standing at the door with a box full of greens clutched in his soil-stained arms.

"Oh wow! Is that from the garden?" Holly knew full well where it came from, but the quiet scientist had spent every waking hour working the soil in the small dome to become something useful.

A shy moment of happiness lit Nathan's face. "Our very first harvest. Make something amazing with it."

Holly took the box from him and placed it on the table that served as her kitchen bench. She picked up one spade-shaped leaf that shone with a dark-green gloss. "What is it?"

"Tatsoi," said Nathan. "It's a vegetable central command recommended as a quick start. I can see why, it shoots up like a rocket."

Holly took a bite from the leaf and tasted fresh green flavour with a sweet mustard bite. "How do you cook it?"

Nathan shrugged as he left. "That's up to you, I just grow it."

Holly left it on the counter as she continued to unpack, but the glossy green leaves nagged at her. It had to be something special to celebrate the first harvest. She wanted to show Talbot he had made the right decision. She decided to slow-cook some of her small supply of beef and served the tatsoi boiled like spinach.

The first bunch turned out disastrous when Holly boiled it for what she thought should be long enough. The result had a texture something like a slimy green leather that had lost all the original flavour. How was she supposed to cook it? Lintang had never cooked anything like it. There was so much she needed to learn. She started over. This time the tatsoi got a bare hint of hot water, leaving it softened but with still enough of the original crispness.

A few hours later, she plated up for the shift meal. Each plate received a portion of beef in a rich brown stew, and half a bunch of steam-wilted tatsoi. The crew loved their first taste of fresh food since leaving home. Several came in to compliment her as she washed up. Holly felt the warm glow of providing an enjoyable meal to others for the first time since the Blauw Zwaluw. She hoped Lintang would be proud.

Nathan came by as she was packing the last of the plates away. "Would you like to visit my garden?" He gave her an uncertain smile. "We could talk about what you would like to grow for the kitchen."

Holly smiled and followed him to the airtight barrier door that led to the garden dome. The garden had been off limits to all nonessential personnel the last time she was here.

Nathan held the door open. "Watch where you walk, the lights are off because we're on the night cycle. She stepped through into the short tunnel connecting to the dome. Warm, humid air flowed past with a faint, earthy odour of mushrooms. Darkness filled the dome, but she could see well enough by earthshine and the blaze of stars overhead.

Nathan led her to a small bench near the middle of the dome. "I like to sit here sometimes," he said.

She sat and gave a soft, indrawn gasp as she lifted her gaze to the explosion of cold jewels hanging in the dark sky above the dome. When she was a kid, her parents had taken her to Lake Bindegolly in far western Queensland. They had camped in the mulga scrub alongside the Bulloo Development Road so far from people and buildings of any kind. At night, her father would light a fire and play guitar as they lay in the sand and watched the wide swathe of the Milky Way blaze overhead. Holly had never seen so many stars, but it was nothing compared to the riotous explosion of stars above her now.

"Quite something, isn't it," said Nathan. "They don't twinkle like they do from Earth, but it's still beautiful."

Holly's eyes adjusted to the gloom. The garden beds of the dome spread out around them. Nathan pointed out carrots, tomatoes, miracle rice, and a lot more tatsoi. He told her of his plans to expand the available growing space, and the other vegetables he wanted to try.

Holly opened a memplant app to make a note of everything he mentioned. She was going to need a recipe book.

****

The droid's visual feed captured the large yellow frame supported by four black hydrocarbon discs. Wavelengths of ionising lunar daylight cast a dark spiderlike shadow as the droid rocked closer on eight articulated legs.

Metal—confirmed as ceramic reinforced steel. Potential mass, three metric tonnes.

The leathery body reared up as it extended two metallic legs to touch the massive bucket tray at the back of the object. A small hatch popped open on the droid's back and a lidar turret emerged. The surface of the world shivered in the droid's view and gave way to interior detail. Hidden structure ghosted through the object's metal surface showing complex machinery and electrical components that were not in its data bank.

It rocked from side to side on all eight legs, in an almost human gesture of indecision, then turned to the low hills in front of Beddau airlock. '*Potential salvage, scrap metal,*' it said in a harsh burst of machine language.

Four other droids skittered over the crest of the nearest hill. 'Share all information,' they transmitted in unison. The cohort of five droids took up a diamond formation for no other reason than because it seemed logical to do so.

'…*confirmed salvage potential.*'

'*Significant refined metal source.*'

Data echoed between them until the oldest, a first-generation model, dug back into its original data banks. '*Identified. Defunct human mining vehicle.*' The older droid switched to a lidar view and spent a full two seconds scanning the derelict truck. '*Suitable for transport use once rectified.*'

'*Strategic logistical acquisition,*' said all five in unison.

Chapter 13

Time Away

Holly lay on her bed and shivered. The heat sink was running down as they reached the end of the two weeks of lunar night. She flicked through her memplant and grumbled about the lack of a network. The communication specialist limited connection to Earth to one burst a week for private crew messages. What was she supposed to do with her free time? The base looked big, but after a week, she knew every corner, almost like a giant grey, stone goldfish bowl. She could connect her memplant to the base network, but it had the most boring collection of technical databases. She would have loved to stream a few shows or play a game, she would even have been happy to download a cookbook. Anything would be better than this.

Holly activated her small memory store and used her memplant to dictate a mail to her mother. It had been too long since her last email home. She wanted her mum to know she was safe and hoped that she would be proud of what her daughter had achieved. The mail would be so much more awesome with pictures. She got up and walked over to snap the kitchen and garden.

Jenkins sat in Talbot's office, discussing supply runs as she entered. The commander glared at her. "Yes?"

"I'm bored. Can I take a walk along the mining track?" She gave them her most hopeful look.

Jenkins glanced at the commander. "Safe enough, the engineers do it every day."

Commander Talbot scowled at her with the universal expression of over-busy people. "Alright, stay on the track and don't go any further than the mine entrance."

Holly gave an incoherent shout of joy and ran to the entrance. The enormous metal shutters of the new airlock filled the end of the passage like a giant iris big enough to accommodate a lunar buggy. She found her suit in the locker alongside the airlock, ready to put on in case of emergency. Slipping her legs into the crinkled organometal suit, she quivered with the excitement of doing anything without supervision for the first time in ages. Her helmet sealed with a soft clunk as she carried out the last of the checks that Jenkins had taught her. The rattle and hum of base machinery faded and were replaced by her own soft breathing.

The blades of the inner door of the lock slid open when she pressed the green button. She stepped inside, and the door closed behind her. Her suit puffed up as a red light came on indicating the vacuum pumps were draining the lock. The outer door irised open onto dawn on Plato Crater.

Shadow still cloaked the base, but high up, the peaks of the rim range already glowed a blinding white in the sunlight. Orange pickets outlined the path to the mine as it angled away to the cliff face. She blinked to take one snap of the view across the hills then started toward the mine. Walking in the low gravity was like bouncing around in a swimming pool. Every step made her soar a little before she settled back to the path. Holly giggled. If she was careful, she could fly like the cartoon princess she remembered from her childhood. She made a short note to tell Mum about it and bounced toward the dark opening of the mine using overexaggerated balletic steps.

The shadowed cave entrance gave nothing away. The mining droid burrowed deep inside the cliff face, returning every four hours to stack raw ore or dump tailings onto the huge pile growing to her left. She considered stepping into the mine but decided not to tempt the commander's wrath. What if something happened?

The bright terminator line of sunshine had crept a little further down the slope. Holly could make out the top of the base from where she stood, but a slight rise in the path hid the bulk of the building. Holly frowned, she wanted to show Mum the whole base.

A dull pile of orange and black mine tailings lay in a heap three times as tall as Holly. It could work, but the unstable, loose gravel looked dangerous, and there was always the chance the mining droid would be back to drop off another load. Beyond the tailings, a break in the cliff came down in a gentle slope. If she climbed that she could get a great snap. If she did and someone caught her, Talbot would send her home for good. Scanning the area around the mine, she checked the path leading back until she had satisfied herself that no one was near.

She took a deep breath and stepped over the white pickets. Other footprints dotted the dust, some led off towards the slope. She followed those, thinking the crew must have gone the same way at some point. The footprints ended near the top of the slope. The view was amazing, but Holly wanted the perfect snap. She walked the small distance to the top of the cliff. Below her, the dark block of the base stood clear of the rolling grey plane—the garden dome glittering alongside in the early morning light.

Satisfied, she turned to walk back down, and froze. A hulking metallic spider blocked her way. The bulk of its menacing body contained barrels that looked a lot like police guns on Earth. She did not move a muscle as a hatch in the droid's back popped open to allow a stubby tower to extend. Holly tried to keep her legs from shaking. This had to be one of the battle droids the commander was so worried about. Behind the grey body the top of the base glittered in the sun, as distant now as another country. If only she hadn't snuck out here.

The droid raised one foreleg and waved it at her.

Her memplant rang. Something it had not done since she got to the moon.

'*Identify yourself.*'

"I… I'm Holly," she said, unbridled terror making it hard to focus enough to transmit through her memplant. "Who are you?"

'*Sigma cohort delta.*'

She did not think the droid was one of theirs, the q-fabs made nothing this scary. "Are you from Chang'e base?"

'*Negative, sigma battalion is no longer stationed there.*' The droid waved its claw again. '*Sigma battalion will trade rare earth metals for refined beryllium ore.*'

Holly gaped. "You want to buy stuff from the mine?" She dared to breathe. "I don't know if we have any of that chemical."

'Supply of beryllium confirmed by surveillance. Stockpile located near mine.'

Surveillance? The droid spied on them.

It lowered the small turret on its back and turned to leave. *'Please wait for decision.'* Its body blurred and merged with the grey rock behind it until it disappeared.

Holly watched the small puffs of dust from its feet until they vanished over the ridge. Jenkin's odd phrase came back to her. The commander was definitely going to have kittens this time.

She waited for hours, but the droid never came back. "Please come out. I can't stay here much longer."

'Acknowledged.'

She spun around in time to see the first gunmetal grey leg uncloak itself. *"Hello Sigma Delta."*

'Incorrect. We are Sigma Cohort Alpha.'

"Oh, I thought you were the other one." She blushed, was it rude to think all droids looked alike?

'Sigma Cohort Delta is on recharge, but event log is transferred to Sigma Cohort Alpha. Past discussion with human Holly is acknowledged.'

"So, you are Alpha?"

'No, we are Alpha, other components of cohort are deployed at strategic watching points.'

Holly scanned the nearby cliffs but saw nothing. "I was talking to the other droid about metals…"

'You discussed trading rare earth metals for beryllium.'

"Why do you want Beryllium?"

'Strategic imperative.'

Holly gazed out over the base as daylight painted its upper surfaces. She shivered. The base would be warming up by the time she got back. She considered what she was about to do. The commander would either be ecstatic or send her home. "How much beryllium do you want?"

'All of it.'

Holly raised her eyebrows. "How are we going to do this trade?"

The small turret popped out of the droid's back. *'Decision by consensus required.'*

It took all Holly's self-control to not turn and run as four sets of invisible feet made lines in the dust that arrowed towards them.

A minute later five droids stood before her in a diamond pattern.

Holly stamped her foot. Five against one wasn't fair. Then she smiled. It wasn't too different to the market. "How much do you want for the beryllium?"

Her memplant registered frenzied chatter.

':…collective development.'

'Strategic initiative…'

'…unbounded collaboration array…'

For every fragment of speech she heard, there were twice as many bursts of dense machine information that meant nothing to her.

'One unit rare earth metals for five units beryllium.'

"No way. We don't have that much beryllium that we can just give it away. One unit for one unit."

'Negative. Trade does not represent equity. One unit rare earth metals for four units beryllium.'

Interesting, the droids could negotiate. She kept that thought for later. "What if we meet in the middle? One unit for three?"

'Agreed. One unit rare earth metals for three units beryllium.'

"We've got a deal."

'Transfer at Plato Crater Base upon delivery. Please accept transfer information.'

A file arrived in her memplant listing metals with strange names like yttrium, erbium, and gadolinium along with available quantities of each.

She looked up at where the droids had been and saw lines of invisible feet leaving in the dust.

The walk back down the hill dipped into shadow and cold seeped its way into the suit. She had uncontrollable shivers by the time she made the base and blamed the cold, preferring not to consider her brush with killer droids.

Commander Talbot was alone in his office when she arrived.

She knocked at the open door. "Can I speak to you?"

"Come in, Holly, what can I do for my favourite chef?"

She stood in front of the sturdy metal desk. "Please don't be mad. I've done something you wouldn't like."

"Why am I not surprised?" The commander settled back in his chair and crossed his arms.

"I went a bit further on my walks than you said I could. I wanted a nice snap." The commander's eyebrows shot up. Holly continued before he could say anything. "I climbed up onto the cliff top, and I met a droid." She rattled out her entire adventure in one long rush of breath. "And, I knew you wanted rare earth metals for the q-fabs. They'll bring the first load next week."

The commander froze her with his steel-grey eyes. Holly saw herself on the first shuttle back to Earth. He waited one long moment, then said, "You are full of surprises. Send me the file."

She did and his eyes unfocused as he read it.

"My word!" He stared at her as if she had suddenly appeared before him. "Don't you have a meal to prepare? Better get to the kitchen. Oh, tell Jenkins to pop in when he has a minute."

Holly headed for the kitchen as fast as was polite.

* * *

Yesha's room was bigger than Jonah remembered, and darker. The administrator's suite remained the biggest apartment in a space-constrained colony. The wide expanse of desk was the same, the person behind it could not have been more different. "Can we talk?"

For a moment, Yesha was still the woman he had met so long ago, then the cold and terrible incarnation of the ruling Chens slipped over her face. "Who is asking? Jonah or the Panamerican representative?" She did not invite him to sit.

Jonah sat anyway. "I want us to talk this through. Panamerica needs your helium. They are starving. I saw homeless people sleeping on the streets."

Yesha's direct gaze did not waver. "I will not deal with a people who enslave those I care about. They turned you into a monster, Jonah."

Jonah stared out the window to where a row of helium-laden trucks crawled towards a waiting Jingnan shuttle. "I spent some time with Doaran. She showed me your new weapons. That's quite a group she's training." He turned to her and searched the bright eyes he knew so well. "You're building an army. Why?"

"Why do you want to know?" said Yesha, her voice dangerously level. "Is it you, Jonah, or that thing?"

"How can you ask me that?" he asked, unsure whether it was his voice or the softmind.

"I must. How do I know that this is not some strategy you are compelled to pursue?"

Jonah ran his hands through his hair, unable to hide his frustration any longer. "I don't know how to get you to trust me."

"That's just what that thing would say to win my trust."

"After all we've been through, I thought there was more between us."

Yesha stiffened as though he had slapped her. "I don't know who you are anymore."

He stood and turned his back on her. "I can't deal with this."

"So don't," said Yesha, the hurt in her voice so plain to Jonah. "You may see yourself out."

Jonah tried to slam the heavy door on his way out, but the door's mechanism resisted. Jonah slammed it anyway. He left the administration building and strode down the wide avenue that led from it, feeling like his heart bled out with every step. What was he supposed to say to her?

The train to New Karakorum rattled with memories of his first trip there with Yesha; how she had been his friend when the Moon was still so strange and new. He watched the grey surface go by, trying his best to think of anything but her. When the train docked, he stepped out with purpose. If Yesha would not see him, he could at least go to Lucien's old apartment and pay his respects to the memory of a fine comrade and friend.

He had made it as far as the cavernous receiving hall before Doaran came walking out of a side tunnel. She reached into her bag and extracted two fist-sized fruit that resembled a giant grape. She held one out to him. "Want? Bet you not had perskaw for long time."

Jonah took a bite. "Oh, I forgot how delicious these were. We must figure out how to export them."

She nodded. "Would be good. Huge oversupply right now." She became serious. "You should visit Beddau."

"Yeah, I know."

"Easier now. Wagon train from bottom level of New Karakorum to Beddau market. Takes six hours. Much better than two days walking."

Jonah thanked Doaran and went to join a crowd of tired miners on the lowest level who were waiting for the train. The tunnel to Beddau looked so different now. Gone was the small airlock hidden behind a rubble slope. In its place stood a tunnel wide enough for ten people to walk down abreast. The original small manual airlock was now replaced by a full-sized automatic lock that hissed open as the wagon train drew near. The wagon train was aptly named, not so much a train as a tractor pulling a line of mining dump wagons. The next shift of miners clambered down as soon as the train stopped as did three boys carrying overflowing baskets of perskaw. He hopped in with the others and made himself comfortable as the train rumbled off on its large rubber wheels. Around him, tired shift workers slept where they stood, grateful for the respite between work and the demands of family life.

Hours later, the wagon train rolled up a ramp between the titanic rock columns that held the spaces of Beddau open. The murmur of many voices became discernible over the low drone of the wagon engine. Jonah smiled in anticipation as they drew up outside a market he remembered so well. A small weight lifted from his heart as he took in the vibrant collection of stalls selling baskets of fresh vegetables and barrels of freshwater fish harvested from the ponds on the lower levels. His last visit had been after Wang and his troops sacked the market leaving nothing but rotting food and broken stalls. His mouth watered as the aroma of deep-fried brijo wafted past him. He promised himself a bowl of hot noodles, but only after he did what he must. Walking out of the marketplace to the middle of the Beddau settlement, he made his way to where an imposing two-storey house dominated the neighbourhood. The old council house had a new coat of paint. Inside the machinery of government ground on. He saw Amira discussing matters with two other councillors. She stopped when she saw him.

"Jonah, I heard you were back." Her voice was light, but Jonah saw the pain she tried to hide.

"I wanted to remember some of what we did." It sounded lame, even to him.

Amira bowed her head in a mute understanding of what he tried to say, more eloquent than anything she could have said. She took his arm. "You must be hungry after trip. Come to my home and I will feed you."

He followed her to the house he knew so well and sat at the low table with its sunken foot-well while she prepared food.

"I hope you still like perskaw. We cannot sell as fast as we grow."

Jonah took in the room and saw new curtains in a bright pattern. "Those are new.'

Amira said they were being sold in the market and told him how the markets had changed, how people created new and interesting things every week. "Is as if shackled creative spirit has burst forth after Suffering, desperate to make up for lost time."

"And what of Jokarah? Did anyone stay there?"

"Jokarah is transformed by influx of people. Half of Beddau stayed there once Suffering ended. Gardens expanded to two levels. They claim to produce best rice wine on Moon, but ours is better."

"I remember how we drank so much of yours at this table."

Her face turned sad. "I miss him, Jonah. Every day I wake, and my little nephew is not there."

"I miss him, too."

"He is one with your brother in vacuum grey now." Her face brightened. "Tell me what you have been doing."

Jonah spent two days with Amira talking over the Moon and how the people had been transformed since independence. He left Beddau with a huge crate of perskaw, two bottles of Amira's best Shaoxing, and a promise to return soon.

Chang'e looked the same, but Jonah knew two days would not have changed Yesha's mind. He asked his memplant to check for messages on the base server hoping that he would find kind words from her and a way to start over. Instead, he received a short burst from Rico.

'Hey, J-man. You remember our deal?'

Chapter 14

At Arm's Length

The report blurred as though her memplant shivered. Yesha pushed aside the tiredness and forced herself to concentrate. Sleep had not come as she lay in bed last night cycle, castigating herself for what she might have said to Jonah.

She had left her tears in the bedroom. Today, she must be what her people needed. The empty ache inside her would have to wait until she could set aside her crown and think of Jonah, not the helium-3 he represented. Both Yesha and the empress burned with a fierce need to make the people of Earth pay for what they had done to the man she loved.

Kaden interrupted her private grief by walking into her office unannounced. "I've got great news."

Yesha composed herself as best she could. She did not rise but fixed him with the glare her uncle had reserved for people who annoyed him. Kaden was becoming far too bold. "Could this briefing not have waited for our regular meeting?"

Kaden had the grace to remember he was speaking to the empress of the Moon. "Forgive me, Lady, but I thought you would want to hear."

Yesha suppressed her irritation and waved him to a seat. "Make it quick. I am in the middle of something."

"The first train from Beddau to Chang'e arrived this morning, bearing a full load of fresh fruit and vegetables. It took two hours instead of six and carried ten times the load of the wagon train."

"Excellent. Please arrange for a consignment of Chang'e silk to be on the first train back. The people of Beddau will love that."

Kaden bowed his head. "I'll make it happen. It will be easy now that the rail line is operational. We've also made progress on the junction to Jokarah." He hesitated before continuing. "The teams outside Beddau have reported seeing droids. There is talk of the droids attacking a crew of four."

Yesha studied the back of her hand. "If the droids attacked, there would be no one to tell us about it."

"Even so, are you sure it was a good idea to let a group of autonomous battleminds roam free?"

Yesha remained silent until long after Kaden had left. She craved the solitude to nurse her feelings, but Kaden's droid story needed further investigation. She told Elizabeth to cancel the rest of her meetings for the day and walked off in search of her exposure suit.

Hours later, her hydrogen buggy tore across the last of the dust plain towards the Apennine Bench. Even from this distance the scale of the droids' construction was obvious. High on the ridge a skeletal tower strained against the black lunar sky. Mining dumps littered the foothills below the tower. Deep in the shadow of the cliff where she had last seen them, frenzied activity stirred up clouds of dust from the gaping hole of an opencast mine.

As she approached, she noticed rows of low buildings that were little more than perforated aluminium screening with a sheet-metal roof to shield against meteorite strikes. She parked the buggy and walked to the nearest building, a rambling warehouse under which dozens of droids worked in a tireless assembly line. A cohort skittered toward her.

'*Benefactor, how will these units assist you?*'

"What are you doing here?"

'*Consensus of opinion. Enable in-country preparation of strategic capability.*'

She looked up at the tower in the ridge. "What is the tower for?"

'*Required collateral for establishment. Communications link.*'

Yesha perceived a tight burst of machine language emanating from the droids' makeshift factory. The cohort in front of her changed orientation so that the diamond no longer pointed at her. '*Additional need for organic components. Require genetic manipulation toolkit and growth matrix.*'

That was unexpected. "You want me to give you a gene kit?"

'*Not give. Trade for aluminium beryllium metal-matrix composite sheets. One metric ton.*'

Yesha understood the value of what they offered. The trade was so one-sided it could have been a bribe. "I agree. When will you deliver?"

'*Sigma Battalion will signal Chang'e base.*'

She raised her eyebrows. Their signal tower would be the most powerful surface transmitter on the Moon if Chang'e was within its reach. If they sent, they had the technical capability to also receive. She made a mental note to check the security status of the Chang'e softminds when she returned.

The eight-hour drive back gave Yesha time to think. The droids were autonomous battle minds designed to establish a military capability wherever Jingnan deployed them, but who were they fighting for now? Their rapid development supported a hidden strategy. Was their original code from Jingnan driving this behaviour or perhaps some remnant of the corruption they underwent during the Suffering?

* * *

Holly ran the makeshift peeler down the carrot frowning as the skin came away in a mangled chunk. The guys had cajoled a q-fab into printing the peeler without having a template file. It worked, but she intended to scrap it as soon as she could book space on a delivery shuttle.

The lump of peel dropped into the collecting bin. Nathan got far too much of his precious carrot crop back as compost.

"Evening, Sprout. What's for dinner?" Jenkins' broad frame filled the narrow entrance to the kitchen.

She rounded on him, brandishing the vegetable peeler like a weapon. "What did you call me?"

"Well, you're always working with vegetables." His amiable grin held no apology. "Why don't you take a break? We're all watching the first shipment get loaded."

Holly cleaned her work surface then followed him to the main living area where Commander Talbot and several of his men were clustered around the slit windows.

"This is a great day," said Talbot. "In thirty-six hours the first helium-3 from Plato Crater will power lights all over Europe."

Holly nudged up to a window in time to see two suited

figures roll a trolley laden with cylinders across the flat to where a shuttle waited. They wrestled the cargo up the narrow ramp and disappeared into the hold.

The commander turned away from the window. "Show's over. Let's get back to it."

The crew gave good-natured groans as they headed off. Talbot gave them a pensive look. "Holly, I think we need to celebrate. Plan us a fancy dinner, something that the troops will love, whatever you like. Just get me to sign off the manifest before you order."

"A great day," he said again as he walked past her. "Now, if only those friends of yours would deliver."

"Friends, huh?" Jenkins gave her a light nudge in the ribs. "Did you really meet battle droids? Most of what I've heard said you'd be spread all over that hill if you had met them. You sure you didn't imagine it?"

"I saw what I saw. You don't have to believe me, but we did a deal."

"How do you know it wasn't a trick? Those Jingnan droids have social engineering capabilities. They can lie as good as any soldier."

Holly shrugged. "I trust them."

Jenkins shook his head as he walked away. "No droids around here. That's all I'm saying."

She watched him leave. What if he was right? The droids had never said when they would deliver. The commander would be so disappointed if she had this wrong. She had to know. Holly went in search of her exposure suit.

***

The train rolled toward New Karakorum. Jonah was so wrapped in his thoughts he did not notice the passage through the hills until the train docked in the gloom of the receiving bay. He wanted to see Yesha, to talk things through with her, but Yesha was away and no one would tell him where she was. The rhythmic clang and rattle of heavy machinery accompanied him as he walked over to the elevators, intending nothing more than fulfilling his original plan to visit Lucien's old apartment. The quiet of the lower tunnels would give him the peace he needed to think about how he could make things right with Yesha, and to worry about Rico's message, whatever that meant.

Halfway across the receiving bay, he looked to his right and saw Doaran's hopper standing in a pool of light. Doaran said the ungainly vehicle could travel fast. Jonah eyed it speculatively. Now there was a way to get some peace and quiet.

Jonah strolled across to the mining service sheds to see if he had a chance of finding an exposure suit. It took no more than a few minutes before he directed the hopper through the main airlock. He squinted in the bright light of early morning and was soon grateful for the lightweight aluminium sunshade above the seats. Before him, the railway stretched through the low hills to Chang'e. He looked over his shoulder at the airlock set in the foothills of the Montes Alpes. Behind the magnificent mountain range lay the monastery of Alsatia. Brother Amos would have an answer for him; the old monk was as close as Jonah got to a spiritual adviser. The hopper battery showed a full charge and it would keep charging as long as he stayed in the sunlight. He speculated on the hopper's climbing abilities, but decided not to tempt fate, and instead take the long way around the mountains to the great chasm that lay beyond.

Jonah edged the throttle up towards maximum power and soon had clouds of dust rising behind the hopper's legs as it made its ungainly gallop across the grey plains. The ride was not so much uncomfortable as strange. Jonah likened it to a cross between riding a horse and sailing on a rolling sea.

A few hours later he reached the crumbling slabs of the mountain that signalled the entrance to the grand canyon of Valles Alpes. Alsatia and Amos lay down that canyon. He tried to turn the hopper but experienced a strong desire to keep moving ahead and a deep curiosity to investigate what the European Space Agency was doing with their base. Jonah examined his feelings and concluded that the latent softmind in his chest forced him onward. He scanned the horizon and knew he was heading towards the distant peaks that marked the ring of Plato Crater. He sighed, knowing there was nothing he could do. It promised to be a long day. He hoped the European base would feed him when he got there. Lying back as much as he could, he dozed in the interminable hours that followed, assigning a submind to steer even though he knew working the softmind harder would make him much hungrier.

Jonah took control back when the terrain climbed to an upward slope. The hopper performed as well as Doaran had said it would. It climbed the hills with terrifying ease. All Jonah had to do was choose the safest path until the hopper crested the final rise and the dark block of the European base appeared far below.

As he approached, he saw the track leading towards what he assumed was their mine. Aiming for the mine, he hoped to find an easy way down. He reached the crest before he noticed a slim figure in an exposure suit picking its way down the slope in front of him.

"Hi, do you know if there's somewhere I can eat at your base?"

The figure spun around to see who had spoken and let out a high-pitched scream.

"Ow! My ears are bleeding. Turn it down will you."

The figure put up its hands in a placating gesture. "Sorry, I thought you were one of them." The speaker was a young woman. She stepped closer and looked up at him.

Jonah waved and introduced himself. "If you climb up that leg, I'll give you a ride back to base, but only if you can find me something to eat. I'm starving."

Jonah saw bright green eyes and a mop of curly red hair through her visor. She climbed up and sat next to him. "You couldn't have chosen a better person to ask. I'm Holly." She tapped his shoulder with one padded hand. "Take it slow. There's a base full of marines down there just itching for a fight with Chang'e."

Holly tried her best to convince the base team to let Jonah in, to no avail. He waited outside the airlock until a trio of burly marines escorted him to the base commander, a resolute man who eyed Jonah with suspicion.

"I know who you are, Mr Barnes. What kind of trick is Chang'e up to?"

"I was just testing the hopper." Jonah held up his hands. "The Empress has enough problems without worrying about a base on the far side of the hills."

The commander's eyes narrowed as Jonah's voice took on an emotionless tone. "I've been back to Panamerica. Earth needs helium." Jonah swayed as his blood sugar dropped further. He tried to focus. If the commander arrested him, no one would know where he was. "I'm carrying no weapons, and there's nobody else with me. The only threat here is a hungry man."

The commander stared at Jonah for a long moment then reached some internal decision. "Jenkins, take Mr Barnes to the dining area and see he goes home as soon as he's eaten."

Jenkins marched him to the table where Holly was dishing up shift meals. She turned out to not only be a great cook, but also good-looking once she removed her exposure suit. She served the shift chicken in a fragrant curry sauce with a side of golden miracle rice.

"You like my yellow chicken curry?" she asked as she elbowed her way in next to him.

"It's delicious."

"You sure that's not just your empty stomach speaking?" There was a decidedly impish cast to her smile as she gave him a gentle shove. "I think I heard it growling while we were on the hopper."

Jonah nudged her back. "There's no atmosphere to transmit the sound. You can't hear things outside, unless it's memplant to memplant on the suit communication system."

"I learn something new every day," she said with her eyes wide. "Come and help me wash up."

Jonah picked up the nearby plates and followed Holly. Jenkins came close behind, carrying his own stack of plates. The big marine had no intention of losing sight of him.

Holly took Jonah's plates. "How does the commander know you?"

Jenkins snorted. "Holly, this guy is the one who turned the lights off." Handing his plates to Holly he locked eyes with Jonah. "I've seen your dossier. That's quite a record you've got."

Jonah's softmind began calculating attack vectors as his feet shifted into a fighting stance. Jenkins rose onto the balls of his feet, his hands hanging loosely at his side.

"Enough testosterone," said Holly, springing between

them. "Play nice or I'll have to stamp my little feet."

"Sorry, Holly," said Jenkins, relaxing his stance. He gave Jonah a quizzical glance. "Looks like you've had martial arts training."

"You could say that." The softmind kept Jonah ready. He forced himself to relax; adding the European team to Yesha's list of enemies was in nobody's interest. "My brother and I reached practitioner grade in Krav Maga."

"Really?" Jenkins leaned back against the stainless steel bench. "Heard that Israeli style can be quite brutal."

"I love it. It's so efficient compared to the traditional styles."

Holly gave a dramatic sigh. "Leave two men alone for five minutes and they start talking sports."

Jonah laughed, and he saw Jenkins smile with him.

The marine clapped a hand on his shoulder. "Come on, I better walk you to the airlock before the commander gets excited."

Later, Jonah dozed as the hopper made its way back to New Karakorum. His heart leapt when he saw the domes of Chang'e glittering in the distance and knew that he was getting closer to Yesha. Setting a submind to steer, he settled back to think through his visit to the European base—Holly's impish smile kept on surfacing in his thoughts. Jonah fell asleep with one question running through his mind. Was he attracted to Holly or was the softmind up to something?

Doaran was waiting when he returned the hopper and she was not happy. "You take hopper without asking. What if hopper was required for emergency?"

"It was something I had to do."

The bag over her shoulder and her damp hair said she had come from training. Jonah thought it wise not to ask while she stood, glaring at him.

"Does not impress me. Can you at least tell me where you went?"

"Of course," he described the trip to Plato Crater and meeting Holly and the crew. "You should see how this thing climbs. It's amazing."

"That's good," she said. "Was no time to test hill climbing so far. Glad test worked out for you."

* * *

"Was the spring air warm upon your skin?"

Seun Fa smiled at Guardian's soldier avatar. "The morning sun is as honey to the starving." He summoned a memory pack containing the business of the day, but Guardian was not done with his commute yet.

"Did you walk or ride the transit system?"

"Today, there is a cold north wind, so I afforded myself the extravagance of an autocar."

The immense political and computing power held by the committee came at a terrible cost. Seun wondered, not for the first time, if he would ever be ready to surrender his body and the simple pleasures the committee longed for. It must be incredible to extend your consciousness through the entire Jingnan network, or to see the world through the eyes of an army of droids, but would that be enough to pay for giving up the pleasure of holding someone's hand?

"What does it feel like, Guardian?"

"There are senses no human body has ever experienced which are sometimes worth the price of duty." The ageless soldier gave him a faint smile. "I was old when I incarnated. I no longer experience the aches and pains of a feeble body."

Seun felt honoured. The committee's paranoid desire for

secrecy meant they never shared confidences.

The other two committee members joined them.

"To our first order of business," said Seun. "The food riots in Kampong economic zone. The mainstream press issued seven opinion pieces critical of the ongoing instability over the last three days. The situation is also trending on social media."

"We must prevail," said Architect. "The cost of failure threatens us all."

"I have taken measures to ensure compliance," said Guardian. "I dispatched a battalion of the new generation battle droids to enforce civil obedience and have a submind running search and pacify teams as we speak."

Foreman glowed amber around the edges of his avatar. "This is the first of what will be many minor insurrections. As long as we fail to solve the overriding problem of the energy crisis, there will be those who seek to find their own answers. Kampong is nothing compared to what will come if we do not prevail."

The subtle whir of air filters maintained for Seun's sole benefit displaced the silence in the meeting room.

Architect passed out purple data oblongs. "I have performed a deep regression analysis of the depletion of Jingnan's helium-3 reserves and extrapolated the overall impact on trade and commerce. The most optimistic projections still leave Jingnan in crisis. The food riots will continue."

"Could we not source alternate supplies?" asked Seun.

Architect passed around another oblong. "We mined out Earth's own limited supply of helium-3 in the early days of the fusion energy boom. There is an exceptionally expensive technique to manufacture it, but it contravenes almost every environmental protection we have. The Moon is the only viable source, and that means accepting what we can get unless we locate another source."

"There is the small European mine in Plato Crater," said Architect. "Projections are that they will produce enough helium-3 to serve Europe."

"Then Jingnan will seize it," said Foreman.

"I do not think that is wise," said Guardian. "Direct military action will lead to conflict with Europe."

Seun's memplant sensed stray packets of data being swapped between the committee as they considered options. "We could outsource the action to our contacts in Panamerica," he said. "I know the Trinax Lobos did not accept the contract to eliminate Barnes, but their drug trade sows chaos in their own communities."

"Flood the European base with cheap drugs," said Architect. "If this works, we will weaken the command structure to the point where Europe will be grateful for the strength of a Jingnanese military intervention."

Volumes of data shifted between the committee.

"Yes, a military intervention followed by an extended period of martial law to promote order and stability." Guardian's avatar looked enthusiastic. "Impressive idea, Seun. This could go on for years. We could even foment occasional minor insurrections to maintain the rationale for military rule."

"To the greater glory of Jingnan," said the entire committee in unison.

Seun checked the agenda. "That concludes our business for today."

Architect and Foreman's avatars faded to nothingness, but Guardian's remained there.

"Do you require something else from me, Guardian?"

The translucent soldier's avatar regarded him with grey eyes. "Your suggestions today have been inspired. I have discussed this with the other two, and we have decided that the time has come for your incarnation."

"But, who will serve as your interface to the people?" Seun tried to keep the welter of conflicting emotions from showing on his face.

"We will find another to take your place. Go home now. Embrace your loved ones. Feel the warm breeze upon your skin and try to remember it."

Chapter 15

Assembly

Four guards dressed in the dark-grey uniform of the Fist of Chang'e stood outside the door to Yesha's rooms. They did not smile as Jonah approached and reached for the door. He had to know. A week had passed since his return from Plato Crater without a word from her. "I need to talk to the Lady."

A grey-gloved hand stopped his. "I would rather not use this on you, but Lady not want to be disturbed."

Jonah looked down into the snub barrel of the lattice trap the guard had aimed at him. Internal attack warnings screamed through his mind as the softmind urged him to get away. He resisted as he scanned from left to right and saw four faces resolute in carrying out their orders. "Just me? Or everybody?"

The guard shrugged.

A wave of confused emotion surged through Jonah as the softmind generated an overwhelming compulsion to see Holly again. Jonah fought the urge with everything he had, desperate to see Yesha one more time, but his traitorous body turned and walked away. Over an hour passed before the softmind released him in the New Karakorum receiving bay. He stood, shaking, until Doaran strolled over from the group she was training.

Jonah waved to her, trying hard to ignore the threat frame the softmind had drawn around her grey uniform. "I can't see Yesha."

Doaran's face remained blank. "Orders from Lady. No help for you."

"C'mon, Doaran. After everything we've been through together?"

"I am sorry Jonah, I cannot help." Her eyes stayed hard, but her mouth betrayed the faintest hint of a conspiratorial smile.

"What am I going to do?" His eyes flicked to where the hopper gleamed in a dull pool of light. "Maybe I should go stay at the other base for a while. At least they're friendly."

Doaran's eyes softened. "I will check on maintenance sheds." She turned and walked away then looked back at him and pointed at a vacuum-sealed crate. "Take sample of Beddau produce with you."

Jonah gave her enough time to be able to honestly declare she could not see what he did.

Minutes later, the hopper ambled across the low hills with the large crate secured across the seats behind his. He had travelled a long way from Chang'e before he realised how subtle the softmind had been in steering him toward Plato Crater.

Jonah's shoulders ached by the time the brooding slab of the European base came into view. Harsh arc lights flooded the exterior of the base in monochrome shades. To Jonah it appeared the same as in daylight, a dark-grey monolith on the lighter grey dust. He edged the hopper forward through the darkness and it clambered down the slope towards Plato Crater.

He stopped outside the airlock and lifted the airtight crate from the passenger seat. The bulk fell against his chest as he climbed down the leg, the crate almost too heavy even for his Earth-sized muscles.

The airlock sensed his approach and irised open. Once he cycled through, he found Commander Talbot waiting with five marines each armed with a heavy vacuum-adapted sidearm.

Jonah put down the crate and held up his hands. "I'm unarmed, and I come bearing gifts."

The commander nodded at one marine who scanned the crate then popped the seal. "Safe."

Jonah bent and reached for a perskaw, careful not to make any sudden moves. "I thought you might like a sample of Moon produce. I have fresh fruit and two bottles of Beddau's finest rice wine."

Talbot considered Jonah with the flinty eyes of a battle-hardened soldier, then said, "We will have to upgrade security if we keep receiving visitors at this rate." He reached for the handle on one side of the crate. "Let me help you with that. The sooner we get it to Holly, the sooner we can have dinner."

Holly wasted no time slicing up the perskaw and serving it as a dessert with reconstituted custard. The commander reserved the Shaoxing until after dinner when the crew produced tin mugs with astonishing speed. The dull stone common room filled with happy voices.

"You can bring us food and drink like that anytime you like," said Holly. "The base supply is very limited. If it wasn't for Nathan and his garden, we would be eating packaged meals more often than not.

Jonah raised his mug to her. "We must arrange a trade. Beddau will be more than happy to trade their excess perskaw."

"If only we had something more to trade than a big stockpile of beryllium," said the commander. "We would be so much better off if we could have built the main dome."

Talbot and Jenkins told him the basics of how the mine didn't live up to initial assays. How production had been low and how there was never enough zinc to make the beams needed for the giant spars that would hold up the dome. "Now we're stuck in this habitat," said Jenkins. "We would like to build faster but none of us can control more than a few q-fabs at once."

After dinner, Jonah walked the hallway with Talbot, while Jenkins followed them with a holstered side-arm. Jonah passed the narrow-slit windows, designed to keep out the sun. "Can you see the q-fabs from here?" he asked Talbot.

"There should be three, over to the right, working on a new mine trolley."

Jonah peered out the window and spotted a lone member of the crew in an exposure suit watching the cherry-yellow glow of metalwork being printed. He opened the memplant and reached outwards. The q-fabs appeared as three bright sparks in the network, with another seven, a hundred meters beyond, waiting in a resting state. Further away something much larger and darker connected to the memplant for an instant and shut down. Jonah searched for it, but whatever it was, it had gone.

Jonah turned his attention to the seven and roused them

from their somnolent state. A few minutes later he heard Talbot's soft expletive as all ten q-fabs coasted to a stop in front of their window. "How are you doing that?"

"I have an upgraded memplant," said Jonah.

The commander turned away from the window, catching Jenkins' eye as he did. "I'd suggest you get some rest now, Mr. Barnes."

Jonah did not miss the way Jenkins pressed in on him. He left the commander and retired to the hard mattress in his small room. The Shaoxing coursed through his veins leaving a pleasant glow, but sleep did not come. Possible futures flooded his mind, the Earth, the Moon, the complexities of interplanetary markets. The softmind perturbed his dreams with wordless concepts.

He found Holly in the kitchen, early the next day cycle. "What's for breakfast?"

Holly held up a cardboard box and read the label. "Peach flavoured oatmeal." She snorted when she saw his distaste. "Don't worry; it'll taste good once I finish with it."

She was right. The crew were digging into spiced oatmeal with raisins when Jonah sat down. He tasted his own and joined the crew in silent eating. The bowl emptied far sooner than he would have liked. He thought it might be the first time he ever complimented someone on a bowl of oatmeal porridge. He took the bowl and made for the kitchen only to almost collide with Talbot who was running toward the kitchen.

"Holly, come quick," said Talbot. "Your friends are here, and they've delivered on your deal."

Jonah followed them to where excited members of the crew lined the walls peering out any window they could find. Jonah squeezed up to a slit window with Holly and the commander and froze when he saw what waited out there.

They were bigger now and armed with an arsenal of death. Stranger yet, they had come by an old truck that one of them drove. "Those are battle droids from the Suffering. What are they doing here?"

"I did a deal with them," said Holly. "Beryllium for rare earth metals."

Jonah stared at her. Only one other person he knew had ever convinced the droids to do anything. "What do you want rare earths for?

"Making more q-fabs," said Talbot. "The internal nanofactory requires a lot of erbium. That truckload is another twelve q-fabs."

Jonah reached for the nearest droid with the softmind and reeled as a wall of military grade encryption slammed down between them. All five droids stopped what they were doing and spun to face the window where Jonah stood. The softmind shut down the link and curled up inside him, almost as if it were afraid. He released the tight grip on the window ledge he did not realise he had been holding.

The droids resumed unloading. Soon the droids had loaded the entire pile of beryllium ore and a neat stack of dull silver bars stood next to the truck. Jonah watched until the battered truck disappeared over a ridge.

"You did it, Holly," said Talbot, his voice ringing with excitement. "That's four shuttle loads of rare earths. We'll be months ahead on the q-fab schedule." He turned. "Jenkins, get the mining team to up production. I want to see the biggest pile of beryllium before those droids get back."

Jonah followed Jenkins to the airlock and chatted as the burly marine climbed into his exposure suit. The European team's suits looked similar to those used by Chang'e, but Jenkins had a different way of kitting up, leaving the wrist and ankle clasps until last. The additional freedom of movement of the European way made sense to Jonah.

"How many more have you built?" asked Jonah.

"Two. It's a slow process; you need two to make one. Terribly fiddly, it gives me a frightful headache after a few hours."

"Sounds complicated. How do you control them?" he asked.

"I don't have to," said Jenkins. "All I do is feed the template for a new q-fab to two existing q-fabs and they do the rest. I just act as the bridge. It's a simple app on my memplant. I'm the meat brain in the middle who watches the feed indicator dials and makes sure the two bots stay in sync."

"Cool. I'd love to see them in action."

"Come with. The commander will be happy if I'm keeping an eye on you."

Jonah suited up as fast as he could and followed Jenkins onto the level area they used for construction. Dull, silver, industrial-scale rows of raw iron and aluminium from the Plato Crater mine lay interspersed with thin rows of the rare earth metal supplied by the droids.

Jenkins summoned two q-fabs and set them to work on the first row, one bot trundled over to the raw materials, while the other set to work on the rare earths. The first bot gave off the citrine glow of nanomanufacture and began to extrude a metal plate for the base of the new bot. The second bot shuffled up to the rare earths and extruded the intricate electronics of a nanofactory.

Jonah felt the softmind reach out to the nearest q-fab and extract a huge file into his memplant. "Whoa!" The softmind proceeded to dump what felt like the books of an entire library into his head. He opened the first file to find the gibberish of a complex machine code.

The softmind reached for the sparks of two nearby q-fabs and set them to work on the next row.

"Hey! What are you doing?"

Jonah lifted both hands of his exposure suit in the Moon equivalent of a shrug. "Thought I'd help you."

Jenkins gave him a noncommittal grunt. Jonah realised Jenkins was at a delicate phase of the assembly. Jonah turned his attention to his own two q-fabs.

Before long, Jonah understood why Jenkins got headaches. The concentration needed to keep the bots in sync was not too complicated, but it was a constant, if you wanted to get the bots into a flow. Each time his attention wavered, one of the bots would end up waiting minutes for the other to complete a task.

He tried to fill his conscious thought with nothing but construction and feeding commands to the q-fabs. Anything to not think of Yesha and the closed door defended by four guards. After working for an hour, he wondered if there was an easier way. He woke the softmind and sent it the construction template. It started a background process that Jonah could only feel in the way subconscious thought presses its weight on the waking mind.

It took most of the day cycle to assemble a single q-fab. At the end, Jonah stopped, exhausted and hungry beyond words, but with a brand-new q-fab circling in front of him.

He badgered Holly for an extra portion at dinner and fell asleep almost as soon as he reached his room. Bright crystalline constructions filled Jonah's dreams and evaporated as he approached.

The next day his head felt swollen and heavy as though the softmind left him with something on his mind he could not quite remember. He gave Holly his most winning smile to extract an extra portion for breakfast then went to join Jenkins.

Outside, on the construction plain, he reached for his two q-fabs. The softmind awoke and seized both bots. It fed them a new program, one Jonah knew without asking was an optimised version of what he had used yesterday. The bots moved forward and began their construction. Jonah felt the softmind using his memplant and realised it managed the synchronisation of the two bots without his direct intervention.

He watched his two bots outstrip the two Jenkins controlled. The softmind told him the construction was forty percent faster and in perfect sync. Across from where Jonah stood, Jenkins' two q-fabs stuttered through stops and starts.

"How are you doing that?" asked Jenkins.

"I guess I'm a quick learner," said Jonah. He watched his own two for a moment then made a tentative reach for another pair of q-fabs. The softmind reached for the new pair with an almost eager anticipation. Soon the second two were at work on their own construction.

Jonah contemplated his doubled output then reached for every spare q-fab on the base.

Jenkins gasped as the bots swarmed onto the construction plain. He finished his own bot in silence then turned to Jonah. "You want my two?"

Jonah stared through Jenkins' helmet to see what the man had not said.

Jenkins waved his arms in a gesture of dismissal. "Take them. You're doing much better than I was. I'll go tell the commander we need more ore laid out." He walked off towards the base.

Jonah added the final two bots to the softmind. He stared at the base wishing he too could be inside, preferably with a plate of food. Giving the airlock one last forlorn look, he turned back to the pile of raw materials and noticed how they were diminishing at a rapid rate. The q-fabs continued about their task. Jonah realised he did not need to watch them. The softmind controlled all the bots through his memplant link.

He headed back to the base.

"Decided to give it up?" asked Jenkins. "You must have a terrible headache by now."

Jonah pointed to the view outside the slit window. "I haven't stopped." He did not wait for Jenkins' response, but went in search of a much-needed meal.

"Hi there, hungry beast," said Holly as she placed a heaped bowl of pasta with snow peas and baby carrots in front of him. "I knew you'd be starving, so I pestered Nathan for some fresh vegetables."

Jonah allowed his contented eating to serve as his thanks. She gave him a wry frown then sat down next to him. "Is it true what they are saying about you?

"I don't know," said Jonah, stopping long enough to draw breath. "What are they saying?"

"That you can control all the q-fabs at once. How many do you think you could manage?"

Jonah put his fork down. "I'm not sure. More than we've got here." He finished his pasta and declined the offers from crew to play cards. The full day of manufacturing q-fabs and Holly's delicious cooking were making his eyes close. Jonah took himself off to bed and soon fell into a deep sleep. Outside his narrow slit of window, q-fabs continued their frenzied construction.

Chapter 16

A Disease of the Heart

Yesha waved to her people as the train coasted to a halt at the terminus within the Beddau airlock. The short two-hour journey from Chang'e to here represented a momentous leap for both places. Beddau, rich in agricultural marvels grown deep within the mountain, and Chang'e, overflowing with electronics and the finest moonsilk fabrics, could now trade. Already her fellow passengers were carrying bags and boxes of goods they hoped to sell or barter.

If only Jonah was here to experience this first journey with her. It had been weeks since their argument, and not one word from him. After their fight, Yesha had buried herself in affairs of state; wilfully too caught up in her day-to-day minutia to notice Jonah's absence. It was only after two days, when Doaran broke down and confessed to loaning him the hopper, that Yesha admitted to herself that she should have had Jonah followed.

The train's glass doors rose with a hiss and people around her waved to friends and family waiting on the station concourse. Inhaling the rich, organic scent of the Beddau gardens, Yesha rose to greet her subjects. She spotted Amira standing to one side with the entire Beddau council. So, it was to be a formal occasion then. She crossed the bright open space of the new station, how different from her first visit in the dust and Stygian darkness.

"Welcome, Lady." Amira gave the brief nod that served as a formal bow for the Moon Folk. "The council of Beddau wishes your indulgence on some minor matters."

No time for celebration then. The council wanted to weigh in on its collection of unattended gripes. A young man spoke of production in Jokarah. Yesha recognised him as the taciturn head of agriculture for the newly formed cooperative. "Lady, we opened seven new fields in Jokarah: miracle rice, field mushrooms, and experimental crop of modified Earth potatoes." He frowned at her. "We need organic carbon. Can't keep up with demand unless we have more."

"Noted. I will arrange for the sewerage plant operators to send processed waste to you. See that you have it transported to Jokarah."

Amira smiled. "Thank you. That will allow us to stay ahead." She nodded to a small group standing to one side. "We have small contingent from Lariah. Survivalists looking to expand."

Yesha waved at the five gaunt people. Individuals bent on surviving the rigours of an abandoned mine would be a resourceful group who would bring new skills with them. One old man glared at her with unbridled hatred. She turned back to listen to what another councillor was saying. One cantankerous old man was not her most pressing problem for the day.

"…people say the droids steal things. Odd items like metal sheeting and ceramic offcuts."

"Do you have any proof of this?"

"No, Lady. We find tracks where stuff was, but never see them."

Yesha had a brief mental image of open metal shelters under the towering mountains of the Apennine Bench. "How do you know it was the droids?" She glanced at the group from Lariah. "People other than you now travel the surface."

The councillor shifted on his feet, unwilling to continue her line of thinking.

"Leave the droids to me," said Yesha, trying hard to hide her impatience with this group of whining supplicants. "Do we have any further business?"

"No," said Amira, stepping forward. "Perhaps you would like to dine with me? We have wonderful selection of fresh vegetables."

Yesha nodded and walked with the older woman to her house. "What was that all about?"

Amira did not reply until they were seated at the low table in her dining area. "People are afraid of your new army. They see groups of uniformed soldiers marching with strange weapons."

Yesha accepted a plate of grilled vegetables. "I'll have a word with Doaran and get her to be more discreet with the troops. She can break them into smaller squads and have them wear civilian clothing. We'll try to make them appear friendlier."

Her old friend looked at her with tired eyes. "Child, they have not forgotten your uncle."

Yesha stared down at Amira's delicious vegetable stew. Her uncle? The dictator who had ruled the Moon with an iron fist until Yesha put a stop to him. She was nothing like that.

Amira turned to lighter topics for the rest of dinner. Yesha promised to visit again soon, and left thinking over what Amira had told her.

On board the train she found Kaden engrossed in deep conversation with the old man from Lariah, in the first carriage. She nodded to them and walked through to the next carriage. As a leader, it was impossible to get everyone to like you, but people like the old man had to learn to respect her. Not because they needed to fear her, but they had to know she was more than her uncle had been.

* * *

Jenkins lugged a vacuum-proof crate into the kitchen and placed it on the floor in front of Holly. "Fresh off the shuttle."

She popped the clasps and squealed with delight when she reviewed the contents. A cryopack of roasting chickens, a large sack of potatoes, and most important, three bottles of French champagne. "He approved it all."

"Hold that thought." Jenkins disappeared around the corner and returned a moment later with a small extruded aluminium box. "The boss told me what you ordered, so I had a suspicion you might want these." He lifted the lid to reveal ten delicate glass flutes that glittered with the radiance of moon silica. "Can't have bubbles without proper glasses."

Later that day, she rubbed fresh herbs onto the chicken, working with as much care as Lintang had taught her. Every kilogram that came up from Earth was a trade-off. Holly wondered what Talbot had surrendered to get the ingredients of a good meal on the manifest.

She paused as it occurred to her that for the first time in a long while, she wanted to do the best she could.

As the hours of the afternoon shift trickled away, faces appeared at the kitchen door, lured in by the enticing aroma of roasting chicken.

"Out. Out." Holly barred the entrance as each approached. "Wait until dinner."

She set the bare aluminium table ensuring each team member had a place setting that included one of Jenkins' beautiful glasses. She wished she had decorated the table with something colourful, but the q-fabs had more important things to manufacture. At least there were glasses.

All too soon the table resounded with happy chatter and the clink of glasses. The commander tapped his glass with a fork and waited until the conversation died. "It's been a tough start, but we did it. Yesterday, I stood outside and saw Europe covered in a blaze of light. Two billion people are grateful for the work you did. You should all be proud. I know I am." He raised his glass in salute. "And lastly, thank you, Holly, for this incredible meal. I've never thought of Plato Crater as more than a base, but with your talents, we can make this a home."

One of the technical team rigged a Wi-Fi broadcast that fed music direct to anyone who wanted to listen on their memplant. Soon several of the crew danced in the open space behind the table.

Holly watched the dancers through half-closed eyes, basking in the glow of a dinner well received. It wasn't the Blauw Zwaluw, but one day, if she tried hard enough, maybe she could have her own restaurant.

***

A week later, the droids returned with two trucks, the second even more decrepit than the first. Jonah watched from a window as the ten mechanical spiders unpacked glittering bars of rare earth metal from the trucks. Talbot was happy that he had increased production; the trucks were packed with just enough refined rare earth metal to trade for all the beryllium ore that waited in an untidy pile for them. Jonah suspected they had been watching and knew the exact moment to deliver the next load.

The crew wasted no time in arranging the new supply into lines for Jonah to transform. It was not long before half the construction plain seethed with new q-fabs. Jonah's softmind controlled the growing population of bots with ease. At least it did so as long as he kept his blood sugar levels up. Holly got used to serving him extra portions. The softmind did not stop working and the collection of q-fabs doubled and quadrupled until serried ranks of q-fabs waited new instructions.

Jonah knocked on the open door to the commander's office. "I've used up the last of the new supply."

Talbot looked up from his files. "I don't know how to thank you. You've saved us months."

Jonah stepped into the small office. "Mind if I sit? There's something else I'd like to discuss with you."

"Look, you've been helpful, but I'm still not sure it's in my best interests to start having little chats with you. What do you want?"

"I had an idea, let me tell you about it and you can take or leave it as you like."

Talbot waved to a seat.

Jonah sat and took a deep breath. "I know we don't have the materials to build the dome, but what if I build you a bigger version of this base?" He pointed out the window to one of the low hills that littered the plain near the base. The one in question stood next to the mine entrance. "I've been thinking, we can use that hill as feed material."

Talbot looked out at where Jonah pointed. "That's a sizable hill. Exactly how big will this base be?"

Jonah had a rough idea, but he instructed the softmind to work it out for him. The answer came back, but, "Big enough to serve as a replacement for the dome," was all he could say. The softmind prevented him from elaborating further.

Jonah left the commander's office with a lot on his mind. Why did the softmind have an interest in the new base? The Panamerican Senate wanted a deal with Yesha. He wandered down the corridor, deep in a reverie about politics and power until he reached the airlock. It gave him an idea. He pulled on his exposure suit and took a walk toward the mine.

He turned off the path once he reached the hill he had been discussing with the commander and took a slow walk around its base. The rear of the hill sloped down toward the cliff face containing the mine. The new location would be convenient for transit to the mine. That should keep the commander happy. The softmind woke and processed a task below Jonah's level of conscious awareness. He felt it access his memplant and spun around to see what it was communicating with.

Smoke rose from the construction plain. That made no sense; nothing burned in the near vacuum of the lunar atmosphere. Jonah peered at the plain. The passage of an entire swarm of q-fabs making its way to the hill kicked up clouds of grey dust as it approached. Between the q-fabs, other machines stirred the dust: automated diggers, gravel sifters, and a dump truck from the mine.

Jonah shrugged and took a meandering walk back to the base. Whatever was being built now, was beyond his ability to control. Back in his room he composed a note to Yesha to say his commitments to the new base would keep him at Plato Crater for a long time. It felt like the right thing to do. Yesha didn't want to see him.

Two days later, Jenkins came to speak to him. "Have you seen what you're building?"

Jonah shook his head. There was no point.

He grabbed Jonah's shoulder. "You want to see this."

They took the short walk to the hill where streams of q-fabs swarmed across the foundations of the new base. The hill had shrunk by an appreciable amount as raw lunar regolith flowed from diggers to teams of bots located at fixed points around the perimeter of the new base. A row of makers, wider than Jonah could reach with his arms printed a wall by sintering regolith into a solid slab.

The two men stepped between the crowds of busy robots as they climbed the hill. Below them, the foundations of the monstrous base had become plain. Jonah traced the outline that ran all the way back to the cliff.

"Going to be quite something," said Jenkins.

Jonah agreed. The softmind had grand plans.

* * *

Dust gave them away. Five shadows ghosted across the low hills to the East of the Plato Crater base, invisible, but for the minute puffs of dust their feet raised as they walked. The new chassis was a design the droids extracted from a hidden Jingnanese military database. Military stealth technology made the elegant octopod body imperceptible to heat, light, and simple lidar vision, but it did not make their footprints invisible.

The link authorised by the benefactor provided significant tactical advantage. In-country information gave the cohort the skills to mine the Apennine Bench and manufacture ordnance.

The design also specified an upgraded battlemind. The tool needed to do that lay beyond the low ridge in front of the invisible five.

'Commence reconnaissance.'

The five spread along the ridge recording the unrestrained explosion of construction happening nearby. The new base was of interest as a potential target, but not their main objective. Each droid extended a high-gain antenna and listened to engineers from Plato Crater base coming and going as they instructed a group of twelve q-fabs to manufacture tools and fittings for the base.

The droids waited with the patience of machines, recharging laminar power cells as the lunar day lengthened. Engineers came and went as shifts changed. The droids remained immobile, listening to a hidden language only they knew.

The sun had touched the lip of the hills marking the crater edge before a short burst of machine language bounced between them. *'Pattern verified. Validate.'*

Twelve seconds of computation followed before all five droids said, *'Confirmed.'*

Over the ridge, the q-fabs stood in a neat row, abandoned between shifts. One q-fab turned a tight circle then moved left and right almost as though it was a small animal questing for food. The small animal skittered along the row of silent q-fabs until, as if sensing an approaching predator, it veered away and rolled up the low ridge towards the droids.

Chapter 17

The Terror of Becoming

Loud rapping on the flimsy aluminium door rattled around the kitchen. Holly sighed and tried to ignore it. The crew could wait—the pile of baby carrots on the metal bench needed a great recipe to celebrate Nathan's latest gardening triumph.

"Hey, chef lady, we're off to take a look at Castle Jonah. You coming to join us?" Jenkins' cheerful voice pulled her away from the tattered recipe book that Lintang had sent her. She caught up with Jenkins and three other crew who were heading for the airlock.

She suited up and Jenkins checked her heating coils. Holly did not often venture out in the early hours of the lunar night; it was cold enough in the base. She thumbed the control on her chest and felt a gentle heat spread through the suit.

The airlock hissed open, and they stepped inside, turning on headlamps to light their way on the short path that led to where the hillock had been. She had watched the dark bulk of the new base grow as q-fabs came and went about their tasks but had been kept from looking any closer by the commander's safety rules.

This was her first proper look at the building. Jenkins was right. It did resemble one of the old castles she had visited in Europe. Sheer walls rose to forbidding heights between buttressed columns. The sides ran back into the sheer escarpment behind it and almost matched the cliff in height. Metal turrets above held blinding arc-lights that picked out the empty patch of land in front of the cavernous airlock.

The marines spoke of Jonah as if he was something other than human. How had one person driven armies of droids to build this entire edifice in the four weeks of one lunar day?

Countless footprints and q-fab tracks scored the path between the two airlocks. Jonah had a whole construction army going. She still found it hard to believe he had done so much.

Within the entrance, the scale became even more oppressive. The dark walls were the same as those used in their temporary base, but much thicker, almost as though a giant sculptor had cast them from living moon rock.

Lights came on as the outer airlock door sealed behind them. Jenkins held up a bulky case he had been carrying. "Nobody cracks a helmet seal until I say."

The inner door irised open on a wide receiving bay that ran along most of the front. This was where the explorer buggies and hoppers would be parked once the team had constructed them. Hidden lighting covered the entire bay in a soft glow. Arched passageways led deeper into the building and broad, sweeping staircases led up to the next level from the left and right.

Jenkins put down the case and popped open a panel. He crouched next to it for a minute. Satisfied with what he saw, he rose and cracked his helmet seal. "Looks like it's safe. Take a deep breath of the cleanest air you'll ever breathe."

Holly took off her helmet. "Doesn't smell like anything."

Jenkins took an exaggerated sniff. "That's because there're zero contaminants. Won't stay like that for long once we move in." He took her arm in his. "Would madame care to see the eating and entertainment areas?"

They strolled up the staircase to the second floor and entered an open area with permanent tables printed onto the floor in alternating red and white. Holly gave a small skip of pure joy when she saw the eight small kitchens that surrounded the eating area. "We'll be able to feed hundreds of people in here."

She wandered out of the food hall into an alley of small apartments behind the kitchens. She opened the door on the first and found a room almost double the one she had at the base. More impressive was the compact bathroom and shower. She activated the tap and watched open-mouthed as water fell from the shower-head and gurgled down a drain. She had heard Jonah and the commander rattle on about sumps and water reclamation, but never thought it would mean an end to the hated basin bath. She wandered back into the bedroom and sat on the cold stone floor dreaming of having a nice room like this. It could even have a decent bed. The crew were all holding out for the shuttle run scheduled for next month that would deliver enough biocarbon to print them all a comfortable mattress.

It took the crew almost a week to carry all their gear across to the new base. Crash couch mattresses had been a priority. Holly carried her own over and claimed a room a little further down from the one she had seen on her first visit. She also occupied one of the eight kitchens. The entire crew could sit in one corner of the dining area. It would be a while before it became busy.

One morning after the chaos of breakfast, she was sitting in her room looking out the narrow window when a disembodied voice said, "Hello, Holly. You are looking well."

"Benny! Is that you?"

"Yes, Holly, I am Benny. Commander Talbot decided it was time to install me. The team placed my core in a secure cabinet, but I am present at all wired locations in the base."

"You made it to your new home. That's nice."

"I detect sadness in your voice. Is everything okay?"

Holly put her head in her hands. "This huge base will soon be full of people. The commander won't need me to cook anymore. I don't want to leave."

* * *

In the three months that followed, shuttle followed shuttle to the point where Holly stopped bothering to watch the landings. Once the European Council traded helium-3 for Indian shuttle capacity, the shuttles arrived with monotonous regularity, each bringing another forty people to fill the emptiness of the new base.

The commander had let out the small kitchen stalls around the eating hall to the highest bidder. There had been no shortage of takers. Holly found work as a part-time cook in the Afro-Italian stall. In her spare time, she helped Nathan tend the acre of vegetables that grew within the underground gallery that Jonah had instructed the diggers to create. It wasn't the life she wanted, but at least it meant she could stay on the Moon.

Fragrant aromas of coriander, cinnamon, and dried ginger wafted round her as she cooked. Big M'butu's food was so different to Lintang's cookery. M'butu wanted a profit. He made vat soy and printed meat from cut-rate source materials and hid the cheap flavours with heaps of Ethiopian spices.

Jenkins pushed his way through the crowd as she carried two steaming bowls of penne al berbere to customers waiting at a plastiglass table. "Be with you in a minute," she said across her shoulder to him.

Back inside the stall, she reached beneath the serving counter and brought out a bottle of bioengineered Ethiopian style suwa beer as Jenkins arrived. She winked as she handed it to him. "Perks of being the cook. M'butu won't mind."

"Thanks, Sprout. Your new job working out?"

She shrugged. "Could be worse. At least I'm getting paid now."

"Hey, the commander gave you food and lodging."

"Yeah, but he didn't want me to work all hours." She placed a hand on her hip. "Mamma built this package for better things than frying vat-meat. I should be running a fabulous restaurant."

Jenkins laughed. "Always up with a quick answer. Sometimes, you've got to put your head down."

"Ugh! Not if I can help it."

"You stick to it. A few years of saving and you could set yourself up with a place like this."

Holly looked out across the crowded eating hall. "What's Jonah up to?"

"Keeping busy. Last time I saw him he was designing a nanobot. Reckons if he could get a swarm of them together it'll make the mining much faster."

She wanted to ask more, but Jenkins finished his beer and stood. "I'm off. Got a health and safety briefing for the latest crowd of brand-new engineers. You think about what I said. You could do well here."

Holly polished the counter-top as Jenkins walked off to his meeting. He might be right, but there had to be a better way than being M'butu's dish pig. She glanced at the stalls one last time and promised herself she would work until she owned one.

***

Holly racked cubes and grinned at Jonah. "That's five three to me. You still don't have moon reflexes." She placed the first glassy cube in the centre of their table. "Let's keep it simple —a five level pyramid." Crowds filled the eating hall, chatting in a dozen languages. The place bubbled with the boisterous voices of new arrivals sharing their first Moon experiences. Across from Holly, a mother wobbled in the low gravity as she fussed over three young children at a table.

Jonah held up his hands in mock disgust. "I know when I'm beaten. Want to have a drink at the new bar on level four?"

They walked side by side in a companionable silence as they entered the fourth level. The bar owners had coloured the walls on this level a vibrant ochre. It was not painted in the Earth sense of the word, but rather powder-coated using a compound cooked up by the q-fabs, when they were not busy with more important tasks. Holly thought it looked cheerful.

"Hello, Holly and Jonah," said a voice from the walls.

"Hi, Benny. What's happening?"

"This week we hit a thousand occupants in Plato Crater base."

"Wow! That's—" Jonah stopped in his tracks, his eyes unfocused as if he was taking a memplant call.

"Jonah, you have another presence." Benny's voice held a tone Holly had never heard before. "Intrusion alert…"

Jonah groaned between clenched teeth.

The wall speakers hissed and cut off with a crackle that terminated in a monotone voice saying, "Complying."

"I'm so sorry, Benny," croaked Jonah as though fighting his own vocal chords.

Holly stared at Jonah, her eyes wide with alarm. "What've you done?"

Jonah's face remained a blank mask. "What was necessary."

"Benny!" cried Holly, twisting around, "Are you still there?"

"Negative," came a dead voice from the walls. "This submind is not called Benny."

Holly shoved Jonah hard in the chest. "What have you done to Benny? Where's he gone?"

Jonah stood as still as a stone statue, his eyes just as lifeless.

Holly turned away and ran down the sweeping staircase, her eyes blurring as she ran. Why did Jonah do that? Benny never hurt anyone. Jonah crushed him like a bug. She could still hear the blank tone of the scrubbed submind telling her it was no longer Benny.

She paused at the foot of the stairs. A silent row of surface buggies waited for her ignorant of the aching hole that had opened inside her. She shook her head as if to clear it. Benny was just a machine; a smart machine that had been kind to her.

"Hey, Holly, what's wrong?" Jenkins' broad hand closed on her shoulder.

"It's not important." She shrugged his hand away, terrified that Jonah might be watching her through Benny's network of security cameras. "I'll be all right, I just need some time alone. Will it be okay if I take a walk to the mine?"

Jenkins gave her a sympathetic smile. "Sure, but no more than an hour, or the commander will put me on kitchen duty."

Holly promised to be back as she took an exposure suit from the rack. Outside, the silence of open vacuum made her heart roar in her ears. She took a deep breath to calm herself and looked down the road to the mine. So different to the simple track she had first used. Now, fused regolith arrowed towards the mine entrance. High-visibility orange markers marked a narrow footpath to one side. As Holly stepped onto it a rover rolled silently past her on its way to the base.

The mine entrance rose in front of her far too soon. She checked her memplant and still had most of her hour left. Above her, on the ridge, flecks of rock sparkled in the sunlight. There was more than enough time to climb up and get a decent photo of Castle Jonah and the expanded mine workings. She left the path and began the climb she used last time.

The electronic voice that greeted her at the cliff-top did not surprise her.

'*Greetings, Trader Holly.*' Five smooth shapes shimmered into existence from the bare rock.

"You look different."

'*Progressive elaboration of capability.*'

"You're so weird." She sniffled and turned to contemplate the empty landscape around the base. "Benny was such a nice softmind."

The droids started a shared conversation. '*Subsumed base controller.*'

'*Major softmind noted. Strategic enemy asset.*'

'*Raised threat potential requires moderation.*'

Holly tried her best to follow the hive mind's parallel conversation. "Wait, you're saying there's another softmind on the base? But, Jonah killed Benny."

'*Not human. Bio-meshed softmind.*' The droids all turned as one to face distant hills. Harsh machine language shrieked discordant notes through Holly's memplant. She opened her mouth to speak, but an answering shriek came from the far hills. Five sightless faces turned electronic eyes towards her.

'Strategic imperative requires trade.'

Holly knew what that meant. "What do you want?"

'Live neural matter, for significant credit.'

"Neural matter? What's that?"

'A brain.'

Holly's jaw dropped. "You want a brain? What are you going to do with that?"

'Random tactical plan requires creativity beyond battlemind capability.'

Chapter 18

Under Countless Stars

Kaden waited for Yesha with two other councillors at the doors to the main elevator. Twenty curious onlookers stood nearby, aware that the mine manager had an important announcement. "I am looking forward to this, my lady," he said, raising his voice to be heard above the cacophony of mine trucks rumbling through the cavernous New Karakorum receiving bay. "We've set it up in the abandoned tunnel on Level Nine."

Yesha gave a regal wave, quite aware of the part Kaden was playing and how she should play hers. "Then show me my new army, Mr Bachmann."

Kaden summoned the elevator and they rode down in silence until the doors opened on a dim tunnel strewn with old mining equipment.

Doaran waited with eight soldiers of the Fist of Chang'e who were dressed in solid, new exposure suits. "Lady," Doaran gave a formal nod. "New suits hardened for vacuum with bullet-proof outer shell strong enough to stop anything smaller than DIRE gun."

"They look heavy," said Yesha.

"Product of Beddau's biovats, Lady. Much lighter than standard suit. Watch." Doaran turned to face the soldiers. "Third finger! Prepare for battle!"

Eight helmets clicked into place as one.

"Two teams of four. First team behind big dozer. Second team hand-to-hand attack only. Go!"

Four team members sprinted behind the decrepit caterpillar tracks. The second team followed a few seconds later and began a cat-and-mouse game of physical combat.

Yesha gave Doaran a small nod as she saw how fast the teams moved; their suits clinging like a second skin despite the bulk. Their moon-adapted Krav Maga style of fighting became lethal to an opponent while the fighters remained safe within the suits. "Well done. This is a great improvement."

"Going to need," said Doaran. "Reports of major troop movements at Plato Crater."

"What have you heard?"

"Have team watching base from hills. Shuttle lands every two days with another forty. Have to think some are military."

"My Lady," Kaden intervened. "We cannot hope to fight against the might of the European Union."

Yesha kept her face impassive. "This is not the time for that discussion."

"My lady, perhaps it is time we made our peace with Jingnan and resumed the helium-3 deliveries. Only Jingnan will keep us safe from the Europeans."

She fixed him with the glare of the empress who had absolute control of her subjects. "Do not test me on this."

The edges of Kaden's mouth turned white as he bit back on a retort.

'Good,' thought Yesha. 'Let him fear me a little.'

She turned to Doaran and said, "Ensure that the entire Fist of Chang'e is fitted with these suits," before she swept past the others on her way to the elevator.

* * *

Subtle white noise hissed from micro speakers arranged around Yesha's bedstead. Earth people told her the cadence of the sound mimicked the susurration of wind on tall grasses, something she had never heard. The sounds promoted relaxed brain states and sleep. It wasn't working. Echoes of the afternoon's argument with Kaden played repeatedly in her mind.

She rolled onto her back, willing the knot in her stomach to go away. The fine moonsilk sheets twisted around her. Sighing, she waved a hand in front of the sensor wall and soft light flared through the dark recesses of her bedroom.

Yesha stared at the ceiling. What could she do? The troop numbers in Plato Crater grew each time another shuttle landed. What if Kaden was right? It was only a matter of time before the European military thought of the civilian colony of Chang'e as an easy target. The droids would have been useful, but the joint battle-mind had opted to stay out of human affairs. Her hollow-eyed reflection in the mirror greeted her as she sat up. The wild-haired stranger she saw there did not smile. Every day that crept past was one more where the people of Earth became angrier while her people stagnated. If only the Panamericans had delivered a deal without corrupting Jonah. Damn them! How dare they use him as nothing more than a tool. She swore as she lay there. One day, the people of Earth would pay for their sins.

Sleep would not be hers this cycle. Yesha got up and sat in front of her mirror. She picked up an ancient mother-of-pearl inlay hairbrush and began brushing her hair—a ritual that took her back to when her mother used to do this for her. Each stroke transported her to a simpler time when she did not have to decide the fate of her people or worry about saving the man she loved. She wanted so much, but more than anything she wanted Jonah back with her, to see his solid presence, and to hear his voice, clear of the empty tone of the softmind making demands.

She walked back and sat on her bed. The unbearable ache inside her became too much until she set all pride aside and placed a call to Jonah, hoping beyond all possibility that it would be him and not the softmind who answered.

The call did not connect, saying the other party was out of range. The memplant service asked if she wanted to leave a message. Yesha caught her breath, glad for that moment Jonah couldn't see her. "I'm sorry. I miss you so much. I don't even know if you will get this, but I want you to know I will do everything I can to make this right." She paused a moment. "When this is all over, I want nothing more than to kiss you under the countless stars."

* * *

The meeting room served as Yesha's concession to informality, the one area where she differed from her uncle. Comfortable lounge chairs and low tables were spread across the open area. Wide arches allowed people to come and go as they pleased. Today, the informality suited her exhaustion after a sleepless night. She sat with Doaran, enjoying a platter of perskaw, tart green melon, and fresh red berries, all courtesy of the farmers of Beddau. It reminded Yesha of her commitments.

"I had more comments from Beddau. We need to make the presence of the army less obvious," she told Doaran. "I suggest keeping the teams small and weapons hidden."

Doaran nodded. "I shall let team know." She reached for a slice of melon. "Was train as quick as they said?"

Yesha nodded. "No more walking for days. You'll be able to visit and be back in time for dinner."

"That is good. I will take small team out there and we can offer to help with gardens."

"Excellent idea. Show the people we are there to help."

"We will, and we keep an eye out for trouble." Doaran stood. "If Lady will excuse me." Doaran closed the door behind her, leaving Yesha alone in the meeting room.

Yesha listened to Doaran's assured footsteps receding into the distance. The wiry woman proved to be a fearsome fighter back during the Suffering; assigning her to oversee the army had been an inspired choice. She leaned back in the chair, enjoying the moment of peace between people bothering her.

A bent figure entered the room using slow, diffident steps until he stood next to her. Yesha recognised the old man she had seen earlier. "You must be one of the hardy folk from Lariah. How can I help you, citizen?"

He stopped in front of her with the same angry expression she had seen earlier. "What gives slip of girl like you right to lord it over free people?"

Yesha frowned. "Do you question my authority?"

Wrapping bony arms around himself, the man burrowed

a hand within his loose cloak. "Administrator left free people, to look out for themselves. No support, but also no rules. Now you come and bring laws and soldiers."

"Would you prefer to still be slaves to the Earthers?"

"No!" he screamed. "People be free." The furtive hand drew a dark ceramic blade from within the cloak as he lunged at her.

Yesha reared away, falling backwards from her couch. The blade hissed past her, tearing a thin line in the synthetic leather. She kicked at his feet from where she lay. "Doaran!"

The man slashed at her again, but she rolled to one side, rising to her feet. "Doaran! Get here now!"

The blade waved from side to side, hypnotic as a snake. Yesha kept her eyes on the blade and the man's shoulders, as Jonah had taught her.

He stabbed at her again, but she twisted to one side, desperate to be away.

Doaran ran into the room with three guards and did not pause. She slid in low, aiming a hard kick at his knees that connected with a sickening crack. The old man fell to the floor, groaning.

Yesha kicked the knife away. "Take this man to the holding cells."

Doaran looked at her, aghast.

"I don't care. My uncle used them for the worst miscreants, I don't intend to differ."

Doaran nodded and instructed her guards to take the man away. "Let me stay with you, Lady. There may be more."

Yesha stood, drawing deep breaths. "I'm going to my chambers."

Doaran fell in beside her as she walked, scanning every entrance.

"I want them all caught," said Yesha. "Every last one of them will feel what it means to test the empress of the Moon."

Doaran remained silent. She positioned herself at the door to Yesha's suite, leaving Yesha to the solitude of her private domain. Yesha stood in the middle of the floor, waiting for her anger to abate. Right now, she wanted the old man dead. She stopped at the hardwood desk that her uncle had imported at great expense from Earth. If she had the old man killed, was she any different to Uncle? Did it matter? Her people had to know her life lay beyond the reach of petty assassins.

Chapter 19

A plague of Rats

The shuttle blew skeins of grey dust off the surface as it touched down. A flexible entry tube snaked out of the arrivals hut and connected with the shuttle. Jonah observed from a window that overlooked the landing pad. Below the lunar surface, another forty people would be making their way along the narrow tunnel from the landing pad to the base. More new faces, enthusiastic for a start in the growing colony. European authorities had jumped at the opportunity offered by Jonah's enormous base and opened the floodgates to volunteers that came from every country on Earth.

The softmind forced him to make a mental note to get the q-fabs busy on the westward expansion then went quiet. It was like having a permanent psychotic supervisor looking over your shoulder twenty-four hours a day. He sighed and walked off to greet the new arrivals. The usual eager faces emerged from the tunnel into the wide receiving bay on the lowest floor. "Welcome to Plato Crater. I know you're all excited, but please take the time to check in at the arrivals desk over there so we can show you where your rooms are."

People streamed past him towards the desk.

"Hey, Jonah." Rico stood watching him with dark eyes.

"Rico, what are you doing here?"

Rico surveyed the crowd. "Thought I would expand my business into a new market—Trinax Lobos used to trade in the Pacific colonies after the Climate war; no legal system or customs officials to worry about. Hasn't been an opportunity like this on Earth for over a hundred years."

Jonah grabbed him by the shoulder. "You're not bringing that stuff in here."

Rico pulled Jonah's hand off and stared at him. "You forgot you owe me? Wasn't so long ago you were begging me to help you."

He strolled past Jonah. "Think I'll go find my room. See you around."

Jonah released the fists he had not realised he had clenched as Rico disappeared into the crowd. The softmind did not identify Rico as a threat. It gave Jonah hope. Rico might be one aspect of his life that didn't interest the softmind. One small part where he was free to make his own decisions.

He walked back into the base, thinking over his options, and did not see Holly until she grabbed him by the arm.

"I know about the softmind." Her hand shook with a fine tremor. "We are going to talk to the commander."

"You mustn't..." Jonah flinched, expecting the softmind to seize control and capitalise on Holly's obvious terror. Instead, it lay silent as they entered Talbot's office.

Holly took a deep shaking breath, preparing to tell

everything, but Talbot already knew. "What the devil are you playing at?"

Jonah sat in one of Talbot's guest chairs, his body rigid. "I assumed control of the base softmind." He slumped in his seat.

Talbot stood and leaned across his narrow desk. "You are taking illegal possession of a registered Eurozone softmind. I'll have you arrested for this."

A wall closed in Jonah's mind and he heard himself say, "I built this base. There are pinhole devices scanning from every corner, all slaved to me. Do you think I can't see everything you do through them? If you so much as consider sending your men against me, I will open their section of the base to vacuum."

Talbot stared at him. "Is this a Panamerican takeover? Europe needs all the helium-3 we produce."

"Your small plans would never feed Panamerica. I took over the softmind so I can expand the base to produce enough for all of us."

"And then, Mr. Barnes?"

Jonah stood and considered the empty wasteland visible through the wide window in the commander's new office. "We will be a credible alternative to the mines of Chang'e." He turned and left Holly and the commander without another word.

* * *

Holly dished up another serve of deep-fried soy to the miner across the counter. "Here you are, freshest Plato balls in town."

The woman laughed as she blinked her memplant to send Holly another credit.

Holly laughed along with her; serving customers was easier than thinking about Jonah's hollow voice as the Panamerican softmind made it clear that Talbot had no choice but to do as it commanded.

She turned back to get another portion from the fryer and twitched as a rat dashed from beneath the cabinet. Everybody had a different theory on how the dirty things had arrived. Holly suspected last month's shipment of flour.

The rat peered at her, its bright eyes puzzling over this strange intruder into its domain. Before she could move, it scurried under a storage container. She didn't have time to think about it, the next customer already stood at the counter. She wiped a bead of sweat from her forehead and got back to serving the fried soy. The hole in the wall she served deep-fried junk from was a far cry from the wonderful dishes she cooked at the Blauw Zwaluw, but M'butu paid her enough to rent a small room and not starve.

Around her, the vast food hall buzzed with the voices of hungry workers getting a meal and a cup of the terrible biovat beer from the stall at the end of the row. So many people, it felt like being back in the market at Maastricht.

Over in a darkened corner, an old woman sang a jazz standard in a beautiful clear voice. Soft soulful strains of melody rose from an acoustic guitar hidden in the dark. Holly smiled at them. Music was like cooking: simple, ancient technology that travelled wherever humanity went. The old couple were another chapter in the flood of people to Jonah's massive base. First came the miners and engineers, then shopkeepers and chefs, and last the crazy dreamers hoping to make it big, like the two making music in the corner.

"Hey, Holly, feeling better?" Jenkins' amiable face appeared across the counter.

Holly's hands shook as she gave him a bright smile. "Want a steaming hot serving of delicious soy?" She beckoned him closer. "I've still got the last of the sweet chilli sauce that Lintang sent me."

Jenkins scooped up the disposable package in one oversized hand as he turned to take in the crowds of off-duty workers enjoying a meal. "More new faces."

Holly nodded. "They keep on coming. I served one of the moon people from Chang'e yesterday. He said they came over in a hopper to sell fruit and veg."

"Get anything tasty?"

"Nah, they sold it all to the big stall at the end. M'butu said it was too expensive." She glanced over at the stream of customers paying top prices for delicious dishes made with fresh ingredients. "Wish I had the money to open a place like that."

Jenkins followed her gaze. "Jonah's built a new extension that goes back into the hills. Think he's starting another mine. There are so many people arriving, you'll get your chance to set up a restaurant."

Holly snorted. "As if! It'll take me years to save up enough credit for that. I'll be stuck in this broom cupboard with the rats forever."

Jenkins stood. "I have to run. The commander's got a list of things for me to do." He smiled back over his shoulder as he wandered off. "You can do this. Work hard and stay out of trouble and you'll be there before you know it."

She watched him walk away. Easy enough for him to say.

As she turned to serve the next customer she noticed a short, dark man staring at her. He looked her up and down as if appraising a piece of meat before sidling up to the counter.

"Hey, chica, what you selling?"

"Deep fried Plato balls, best in town."

The man ordered a portion and stood at the stall eating. "Not bad, I like the bit of spice."

Holly smiled. "Glad you like them. I get a supply of spices from a friend on Earth."

He looked around then leaned across the counter. "I heard you talking to your friend. You want to make a little extra, you could sell a few things for me. Busy stall like this, you could keep another product under the counter easy."

Holly considered him as if seeing him with new eyes. There were men like him in Maastricht, always ready with their little bag of tricks. "No way. I'm not doing that."

He gave her a level gaze as if he saw something.

"That's your choice. You change your mind, you come look for me. Just ask for Rico. We could do business, you and me."

Two day cycles later, Holly found herself scrubbing down the greasy benchtops. M'butu's cheap soy got into everything. The oil cake that formed inside the vapour trap above the deep-fryer, stinking of rancid grease, was the worst. She scraped the congealed mass out with a spoon and tossed it in the compost bin. She couldn't imagine Lintang putting up with a mess like this in her kitchen. Not for the first time, she gave in to the daydream of running her own place. At least it took her mind off the sludge.

A small grey snout poked out from under the storage cabinet, twitching silver whiskers. Another one. Holly took a broom and chased the rat out. It dodged away from the invasion of its territory and scrambled up the rough stone of the wall onto the kitchen bench. She slammed the broom down after it. The rat sprang sideways and landed in an open storage bin.

"Gotcha!" Holly slammed the lid shut, pleased to have caught one. The rats were far too smart.

She set to tidying up the disturbance caused by her attempt at extermination. What was she going to do with it? Jenkins would know.

The rat scrambled inside the bin, Holly pressed the lid down tight. She considered it for a moment, then reached over to a shelf for one of the airtight storage hampers they used to take food to the mine. She had to be quick now.

Holly opened the storage bin a crack and reached for the rat. It gave an enraged shriek and clawed at her hand as she grabbed it. She tossed it into the airtight hamper and snapped the lid shut before it could escape. Cradling the hamper under one arm, she went to tell M'butu that she was on her way to deliver a mid-shift snack to the mine. He waved her off, intent on the work he was doing.

Minutes later, she stepped outside, walking towards the mine. She turned off at the foot of the cliff and started climbing in search of the droids.

Five sombre shapes waited for her when she reached the top, their bodies casting minimal shadows onto the grey dust.

"Hello again. I have a trade for you." She placed the hamper at their feet. The nearest droid extended a small black pillar from its back.

'Live animal.'

'Potential for integration.'

'Suboptimal intelligence quotient.'

Holly waited until their chatter died down. "Do you want it? You said you wanted neural matter."

'Offer two hundred credits.'

Holly sneered, even though it was wasted on these things. "No deal. You said significant credit."

The droid picked up the hamper with one retractable claw. *'Offer stands. Significant credit for living human neural matter without ambulant peripherals.'*

"No way! I'm not bringing you a person." She staggered back from them as her memplant registered the transfer of two hundred credits.

The droid did not follow, instead the droid's hollow electronic voice spoke direct to her. *'No person required. Five hundred thousand credits for live human neural matter.'*

She stopped where she stood and stared at the empty rock where the five grey shapes had vanished for a long time.

The tears came later as she sat in her small room. Holly had always considered herself a good person, but that much credit would let her open any restaurant she wanted.

Chapter 20

Ascension

A row of multihued cottages lined the sombre grey of the accommodation tunnel on Level Twelve of New Karakorum. Each door and window stood out from the matt white of the walls thanks to the iridescent reds and blues of borders around each. An enterprising individual had planted trailing devil's ivy in hanging boxes between the buildings, the glossy green leaves adding to the riot of colours.

Yesha preferred subtler shades but kept her enthusiasm visible. She had come to celebrate the successful completion of the refurbishment and to open the accommodation for occupation. The renovation project had provided much needed work for idle hands. As empress she intended to make the most of praising the workers.

Beaming faces watched her from within the small crowd of refurbishing crew and hopeful homeowners as they waited for her to speak. Yesha did not miss the less pleasant looks coming from a group at the back. She gave a discreet glance to the two Fist of Chang'e guards who kept close behind her. Their weapons did nothing for her peace of mind even though Doaran had insisted on them always being with her after the attack. As unreasonable as it was, she wanted Jonah, his Earther size, and the fighting skills he had shown during the Suffering.

Yesha began her speech by praising the enthusiastic construction and the opportunities for new industry that the renewal of Level Twelve meant. The crowd listened in polite silence, but she kept the tone light and her words to a minimum. She could see they were eager to explore the renovations.

Doaran stood waiting to one side as the scattering of applause died down. "Need to speak." She flicked her eyes to an empty cottage. "Better in there."

Yesha stepped through the door that one of the guards held open for her. Doaran followed, telling the guards to wait outside the cottage. "No one enters until we finish talk."

Dim light filtered through the electrostatic mesh that covered the window opening, illuminating the engineered quartz counters of an otherwise empty apartment. Doaran checked the sleeping quarters and shower, prowling from room to room like a caged animal. Satisfied, she came in close to Yesha. "Enquiries completed into assassination attempt," she said, keeping her voice low. "Nothing useful, but much talk in certain quarters of foreign involvement." Her eyes darted to the door. "I cannot prove, but it could involve one or more councillors."

Yesha stiffened as a chill spread through her core. "Speak of this to no one but let me know if you find anything."

Doaran nodded. "Also, need to deal with prisoner. Too visible to public. Is creating bad feeling in domes. What will you do with him?"

A day later, the gentle thrum of the steering wheel under her hands was the only physical sign of the ancient hydrogen engine working hard. Dust flew from the oversized wheels as the buggy put distance between her and Chang'e. Yesha looked back over her shoulder at the domes containing all her problems. Doaran had argued against her travelling alone in the buggy, but Yesha needed this time away to think.

The wheels climbed a small dune and her aimless wandering took on purpose as the towering cliffs of the Apennine Bench appeared in the distance. She gunned the motor now, eager to get to her answer. The low hills flew past and soon the buggy climbed over the final ridge that stood before the area the droids had chosen.

Yesha slowed the buggy to a crawl as the droid's site came into view. Beyond the ridge, swarms of droids moved across the surface of a serried rank of gleaming towers that no human mind had ever dreamed of. Sunlight flashed across the blinding white of silicate construction. The droids made use of available resources, manufacturing gleaming quartz from the silicon dioxide in the regolith.

Her eyes followed the curve of a great spire to a height beyond the ridge. Beyond it, white-hot reflectors up on the ridge poured molten sunlight into a crucible from which slag metal poured in gobbets of angry red. Motes of light moved about the depths of the vast cavern that had replaced the primitive mine she had seen before. The droids had achieved industry on a grand scale.

She started down towards the city, driving with her mouth

slightly agape, taking in the wonder of a metropolis unlike any other. Five dark shapes drifted out to meet her in a neat diamond formation. She let them approach. They looked nothing like the last droids she had seen. These sleek artifices prowling forward on sinuous legs looked more like Earth animals than the machines she knew they were.

'*Benefactor. How may these units assist?*'

"What happened here?"

'*Progressive elaboration.*'

'*Required strategic improvements.*'

"You needed to build a city?"

'*Defence required extraction of in-country resources.*'

Yesha took in the great spiral of the spire crowned with a transmitter array. Crowds of dark-grey shapes crawled along the lower reaches of the spire.

'*Integration of benefactor resources represents progress.*'

"I only gave you a few old things."

'*Disambiguation of meaning. Integration of benefactor.*'

"How could I join you? This place cannot host a human."

'*A suitable habitat exists.*'

She shook her head in frustration. "Never mind that. Hostiles threaten Chang'e; the Europeans are planning a takeover. I'm sure of it. I want you to enter the base and subdue them."

'*Denied.*'

"What? After all I have done for you. You better do this, or I will have you all terminated."

The five droids spread out in a line. An ominous short black barrel protruded from each body. '*Likelihood of successful termination is minimal for these units.*'

Yesha took slow careful steps toward the buggy trying hard not to make any sudden moves. Back in the seat she started the ancient engine and aimed the wheels back towards Chang'e.

A disembodied voice echoed in her head as she drove, *'Consider the offer.'*

She waited until she was halfway to the domes before stopping the buggy and allowing the tension to leak from her shoulders.

Events conspired to block every path she chose to take. The droids would not help her prevent a military incursion; her council was turning against her; and Jonah remained a topic too painful to even contemplate. She gave in to her self-pity for a moment, but then a bitter smile curved her lips. Her people wanted a strong leader more like her uncle. She could be strong, and she knew where she would start.

* * *

Seun Fa drifted through a white mist, the likes of which had never crossed his beloved Jingnan. The mist brushed his face with its cool breath as though he moved through it, and yet, there was no end to it, or ground below him.

The harmonious ringing of yunluo gongs evoked the memory of a last century China Wind tune Seun had heard in his youth. "Brother, are you ready to join us?"

The fog clotted into a darkness that coalesced into the grey soldier avatar of Guardian.

Seun shook his head. "Is it time for our meeting?"

The grey avatar shook its head.

A thought struck him. "You are a woman?"

Guardian smiled. "I was, but such things are behind me now." She gestured, and two red armchairs materialised out of the mist. "Sit, I remember how confusing it is to be freed of three dimensions."

Seun looked at the chair and found himself sitting without having moved. Guardian sat across from him. "We each have our private spaces. By convention we do not enter each other's space unless we are invited. I hope you will forgive my presumption at entering your space, but I felt you may need guidance."

The haze of anaesthesia cleared from Seun's mind and brought memory to his confusion. "It was successful then?"

"You asked if I was a woman. The thought occurred to you because of your connection to our shared data pool. You will remember what we have learned."

Seun tried to think of what he knew of the committee and gasped as he remembered reams of information. Guardian watched him with a bemused expression.

She made a complex gesture with her right hand. Seun thought it might be more for his benefit than necessary. The mist shifted, and a room formed around them containing Architect and Foreman.

"Welcome, Seun," said Foreman. "Your sacrifice for the greater glory of Jingnan will be remembered in the records of history."

"I am honoured to serve."

"You will do more than serve, you will rule. For all of mankind's cleverness, we are yet to create a machine capable of pure creative thought. We four are the spark of inspirational genius that powers even the strongest of our softminds when needed."

Guardian faced Seun, her face projecting the mask of high office. "It is customary among us to take a new name after ascension. It is your choice, but I would suggest Traveller."

Foreman opened information streams that Seun perceived as rivulets of smoke running between them. "Our agents in Chang'e failed to eliminate the upstart empress. Her security captured the assassin. This minor failure will not stop us. We will bide our time until she makes a mistake. One human cannot stand against the combined haiman intellect of this council."

A cloud of analytical processes drifted around them, too dense for Seun to follow. Guardian gave him a reassuring smile. "Do not fret, little brother. You do not have the softmind extensions we have installed over the years."

The fog dissipated. "Projections agree with Foreman's assumptions," said a disembodied voice.

"This implies that the energy crisis will deepen," said Guardian. "The longer that woman sits on her throne, the less helium-3 we will have available. Food production will cease as our energy stockpiles run low. Millions will starve."

"I have given thought to this emergency," said Foreman, extending a pile of purple data folders to them. Seun's high-level scan revealed subjects he had not heard of before.

Foreman addressed him on a person-to-person link, "While you were only human, we could not share our deep security files with you. An unsecured person represented too many options for leakage. Read these documents for our next discussion."

Seun opened two of the folders and data flowed into his mind. He opened the remaining folders then stopped and stared at the others. "We have a military base on the Moon?"

"Something both more and less than a base," said Architect, opening a scrolling video feed of the airless lunar surface. "During the insurrection last year, we sent to our agent Wang a distributed battlemind. This he installed in repurposed rescue droids which the Chen woman stole. Fortunately, the battlemind can take its own initiative on most things. We spent the past six months in a subtle manipulation of its intentions." The video jittered and swung to show a sprawling alien city glittering against the dark mountains of the Apennine Bench. "The results are pleasing."

Guardian placed an insubstantial hand upon Seun's

shoulder. "This is why you carry no peripheral softminds. Once your training is complete, you will journey to the Moon and seize command of the battlemind and the city the droids are building."

Chapter 21

Ruinous, but Acceptable

Aslick sheen of grey nanobots glistened over the rock surface. Visualising the basalt through the sensors on each bot, Jonah used his softmind to combine reams of information into a coherent whole that he wore like an invisible glove. An unbearable itch told him when the nanobot swarm flooded an invisible weakness in the looming rock above his head. Taking two steps back, he willed his mental glove to scratch the itch. The slick surface folded into the crack, causing the rock to groan as it expanded until, with a soft rumble, half a ton of rock fell forward. Jonah stayed where he was as the acrid gunpowder reek of fresh rock wafted past him. The softmind knew the hail of sharp-edged rubble would stop before it reached his feet. He gave the softmind a subtask to bring in a team of mining bots to harvest the raw helium-3 ore before turning to the next sheet of rock that already shone with a layer of nanobots. The chase for helium-3 had pushed him to reach deeper into the hill. So much so that the base team were already calling the mined-out first segment Shallows and insisting it was ready for habitation.

Jonah brought down the next wall of rock. Satisfied with his progress, he left the mining bots to get on with the job while he went in search of food for his ever-hungry softmind. As he walked, Jonah drew mental schematics of the airlock between Deep and Shallows. With the perfect position, it would keep out dust, making the accommodation in Shallows so much more comfortable.

A shambling mass collided with him. "Sorry, man." The guy licked his lips and stared at Jonah through a tarf-burned haze, his head lolling as though not attached to his body. Nausea hit Jonah as the softmind recoiled from the burning need welling up inside him. He shoved the tarf-head away and stumbled down the corridor while the softmind hastened to form aversions to a hit of his favoured drug in his mind.

Jonah stopped around the corner and leaned against the wall, stilling his breathing to compensate for his internal turmoil. The softmind built walls of revulsion around his longing. Why did he feel it now? It had been so long since he thought of tarf. He needed space to think, somewhere he could be alone.

Half an hour later, he sat on a packing crate hidden in the shadows towards the back of the receiving bay. Around him, the automated transport unit unpacked cylinder after cylinder to the accompaniment of muffled rattles from the precision packing machinery. Plato Crater ore held half the helium-3 of the rich Chang'e lode, but still enough to create rack upon rack of helium-3 canisters.

Rico worked fast if addicts were brazen enough to be seen in public. Burning energy in its need to solve the problem, the softmind opened, analysing the threat to its objectives.

Talbot did not have enough men to watch the expanded base. Rico and his sort would waste no time in identifying low-surveillance spots suitable for trade. Jonah kept an eye on the results as the softmind calculated the number of microcams needed to watch the entire base. Two thousand microcams would need a second softmind; the base softmind could manage that. Jonah shuddered as his softmind weighed the costs of reducing the base environmental controls to free up enough computing power to enable surveillance.

"Why are you sitting alone in the dark?" said Commander Talbot, coming up alongside him.

Jonah rose from his packing crate, unsure of what to tell Talbot.

The commander beamed at Jonah. "We did it," he said, pointing at the squat grey cylinders as they emerged from the unit. "A full production run, and not just enough for Europe. This is the first guaranteed supply of pure helium-3 outside of Chang'e." Clapping Jonah on the shoulder, he said, "We couldn't have done it without your help."

"Glad I could be useful."

"Useful? If it wasn't for your talents, we would still be mucking about in the temporary base."

Jonah shrugged, trying to keep up with Talbot's enthusiasm. Everything the memory of the glass-eyed tarf-head represented kept surfacing in his mind. The softmind's interference left him with a nauseating blend of desire and revulsion, almost as if it could not decide what it wanted him to feel. Instead, he tried to focus. "We should expand by cutting a new level below the deep section. I can get the mining bots to cut a spiral ramp like the ones they use in the Chang'e mines."

"What a good idea. We can go up or down from Deep and follow the richest ore layers."

Jonah focused on the trolley as it lowered clamps over the waiting cylinders. "It might be a good idea if you get your geologists to figure out where the high-yield strata are located."

"Sir," said Jenkins, arriving at a fast walk. "They're on final approach."

"Excellent," said Talbot. "Get the men to wheel these trolleys out to them." He turned to Jonah. "Come to my office, Mr. Barnes, we can watch this historic occasion from there."

Jonah turned to Jenkins. "Hey, did you find that missing q-fab?"

"Nope. Didn't show up anywhere."

"It's weird, it just disappeared from my network of bots, almost like someone turned it off," he said, following Talbot up the stairs. Losing the q-fab was a minor mystery he wanted to solve.

Talbot had improved his office by the addition of three comfortable chairs that must have come up by shuttle. He waved to one for Jonah then turned to the broad window. "Ah, here they come."

Outside, the solid mass of a European shuttle blew plumes of dust as the reaction engines pushed it to a gentle landing. The craft settled with an abruptness that suggested it was being piloted by a human. Jonah's softmind calculated descent velocities and produced an answer that the shuttle's crew were shaken but unharmed. Two figures emerged after the hatchway opened. They waved to the men who were pushing a trolley laden with cylinders towards the shuttle.

"Poor blighters," said Talbot. "It's a touch-and-go mission. They get just enough time to have a cup of tea before rushing back to Earth."

Jonah said, "Uh-huh," to hide the wave of dizziness that swept through him.

"It's for the best," continued Talbot, unaware of Jonah's distress.

Jonah tried to respond, but the room shrank around him, almost as if he drifted down a long, dark tunnel. He heard his own voice say, "Panamerica would like to take an option on the next production run."

Talbot turned to him with a knowing smile. "I was right when I told the Council you were a Panamerican sleeper. They wouldn't believe me, you know, but I had my suspicions when you became so helpful." He sat in the chair next to Jonah. "The European Union is happy to assist the great country of Panamerica. Plato Crater Base can deliver refined helium-3 at two million credits per cubic metre at standard pressure."

The softmind executed a complex macroeconomic analysis of the cost of helium-3 against gross domestic production and lifestyle. The entire process lasted a second and a half. Jonah heard his voice say, "The price is ruinous, but acceptable."

Talbot rose and shook his hand.

"A pleasure doing business," said the softmind.

Jonah turned and left Talbot's office in a stunned silence. The softmind had played him all along, controlling the q-fabs, building the base and mine, fighting his addiction, even his argument with Yesha. Every action had been a step along a path towards the goal of providing Panamerica with a guaranteed supply of helium. It wasn't him. The thing inside him had done it all. Slamming his fists against his chest, Jonah held on to the anger that was his, and his alone. He didn't stop walking until he reached the far end of the mine in Deep.

Muffled clicks and bangs infiltrated the silence of the mine. Jonah stood in the darkness and listened to the sound of machinery cooling and rocks settling around a space vacant for the first time in millennia. The absence of light suited him; the less he saw and felt, right now, the less input the softmind had. Its hard lumps lodged in his chest as cold and dead as two bricks.

His stomach groaned, responding to the results of softmind's demands on his blood-sugar. It must have done a lot of processing, judging by how hungry he was now. Jonah gave brief consideration to starving in an attempt to weaken its hold, but knew the softmind would force him to eat, if he tried. If he had to feed it, he might as well order something decent. Chippers served deep-fried vat steak with a side of pickled mushrooms. He turned on his headlight and went in search of food.

Chippers bustled with a mob of happy customers. Mine workers, flush with cash from the last helium-3 run, mixed with off-duty marines, and a sprinkling of scantily dressed men and women who Jonah was sure had no official business in the mines. A mood of urban sophistication had infected Plato Crater.

Jonah ordered the steak and added a jumbo serve of caramel vat fudge. As an afterthought, he flicked the autovendor a few extra credits for a shot of Chang'e Shaoxin. The chrome-plated hand slid a glass of the straw-coloured liquid toward him. He took his drink and headed toward an empty booth.

Rico strolled out of whichever corner he lurked in. "Hey, Jonah. What you drinking?"

Jonah held up his glass, "Good Shaoxin from the vats of Jokarah."

Rico made a face as he sat. "You gone local, chico? That's no drink for a man."

Jonah shrugged. "What do you want, Rico?"

"Nothing, man. Can't I sit and talk with an old friend?"

A serverbot arrived at their booth. It reached into its bulky midsection with stainless steel arms to lift out Jonah's steak and fudge. It rummaged around in its interior for Rico's order. Jonah ignored it, the softmind demanded glucose with all the subtlety of a ravenous animal. It moderated Jonah's need for food until all he could think of was rich, golden, caramel fudge. He ignored the steak and began swallowing spoonful after spoonful of the sticky treat.

Rico took a scoop of his Earth-grown nachos but did not eat. "You got the hungries? I got a bag that can fix that."

Jonah did not stop until his plate was clean. With the softmind occupied with replenishing itself, he could focus. "I told you I was done with that stuff." He brought his hands up onto the table. "I found one of your customers."

Rico smiled. "Lots of them around now. I got a good bankroll."

Jonah opened his mouth to respond, but the softmind cut him off. He felt the beginnings of returning hunger as the softmind drew hard on his energy reserves. "You have a nation funding you. No other party has sufficient capital reserves for off-world activities on this scale." Jonah blinked, surprised by the softmind's conclusion, but it was not done. "The Europeans and Panamerica would not do this, Central Africa has been bankrupted by the helium-3 crisis. That leaves Jingnan."

Rico stood and stepped out of the booth. "I never figured you for one of the clever ones. Stay out of this, you can't take them on." He placed a hand on Jonah's shoulder. "For old times, I'll give you a bag. Smoke up and listen to that loco music you like. Forget we ever spoke about this."

Jonah brushed his hand away. "Get lost, Rico. I'm done."

Rico looked down at him, "You've changed. You sure that's what you want?" He left the question hanging as he strolled into the crowd, looking for his next customer.

Chapter 22

Exile

Half of Chang'e watched from the sides of the great hall as Yesha sat in the ornate chair her uncle had used for this exact purpose. The irony was not lost on her. "Terang van Dekt, your crimes have been described to all who stand here. I find you guilty of an attempt on my life. Is there anything you wish to say before I pass judgement?"

The dishevelled prisoner glared at her from between the two guards. "I am old man, does not matter. Stupid girl, you not see what is happening."

The waiting crowd listened in a disconcerted silence. Yesha scanned the expectant faces and noticed Kaden sitting with some other councillors.

Terang laughed. "You think you rule Moon Folk, but you don't even know which of your councillors get fat on Jingnan credit."

Yesha kept her face impassive, not wanting to give the crowd the satisfaction.

Terang seized the opportunity and twisted to face the people. "Why you let weak girl rule you? Spends money on grand railway, but no new helium-3 deal with Earth. Dumb people, you deserve the leaders you choose, and you chose badly. Old Administrator knew how to make things work."

Uncertain faces watched her, waiting for her response. Quiet murmurs rose from hidden voices. Uncle had taught her symbols were important. She understood that now. Visiting the droids had confirmed her bitter understanding of what she needed to do to keep control. She rose. "If you prefer the old ways, then so be it. You shall pay in the old ways." She pointed to the side of the hall where heavy glass jars, taller than a person, stood unused since her uncle's time. "Take him away and recover his water."

The old man said nothing as the guards led him to the recovery jar and sealed him in for whatever remained of his life. In a shocked silence, the vast crowd waited, until with a final thump of weighted glass the lid settled echoing her judgement.

Yesha raised one angry fist. "Justice. This is what happens to those who challenge me. I warned Jingnan not to interfere in our affairs." She spoke to the crowd at large, but then looked to where Doaran stood. "I want you to load the rail gun with a slab of fused basalt. Bomb the rocket launching platform in Jingnan."

Kaden stood to one side, looking at her as if he saw her for the first time. His expression a mixture of fear and elation. She knew which one she preferred.

"Start now, Doaran. Aim well and keep on bombing them until nothing but a smoking ruin remains."

* * *

Holly drifted in to work, still thinking through what the droids told her. Crowds of off-duty mineworkers flooded the eating area. She spotted that Rico character strutting around as though he owned the base, stopping in at tables to tap a likely mark on the shoulder. She walked on as fast as she could, but he stopped in front of her.

"Hey, chica, you think any more about our deal?"

She wiggled past him. "Not here, meet me after shift at Chippers, that new bar in Shallows."

Rico grabbed her hand. "Where's that?"

"It's the shallow end of the new section, just walk to the end of the base and go through the airlock." She pulled hard, "Let go, you're hurting me."

Rico twisted her arm harder before letting her go. "Just remember who you're speaking to."

Holly's arm throbbed for the rest of her shift as she dished up one helping after another of the deep-fried soy paste. Her mind turning over what a deal with Rico meant. So many people passed through the food hall, it would be easy to slip the occasional package out from under the counter. The extra cash would be useful, but how would she live with herself? Burned-out narcos shuffled through the Maastricht back streets; she'd met more than one. How could she do that to people? Today brought two offers she could neither accept nor ignore.

By the time her shift ended she stank of protein-enriched soy and the acrid tang of fungus oil. She cleaned up as best she could and made her way from the food hall, down the long corridor that ran most of the length of the ground floor. Jonah's q-fabs had built a wide ramp at the end that ended in an airlock big enough to house a mining truck.

She waited with a group of mine workers until the huge door irised open with a hiss. A bot emerged towing a trolley of helium-3 canisters. The workers shuffled past it and the lock cycled around them. Her ears popped as a dull thud announced the opening of the far side. Rock dust and synthetic lubricants peppered the air with the characteristic scent of lunar mining.

Holly turned left toward a tunnel that sloped upward. Dull strip lighting above the entrance had been bent into letters that announced the dim tunnel as the way to Chippers.

The bar was the latest example of Plato Crater miner hip. Brushed aluminium benches stained a variety of gaudy colours lined dim alcoves nibbled out of the rock by regolith miners. An oversized mechanical autovendor tended the fused glass bar, spinning drink cannisters across to crowds of waiting customers.

Rico slid out of a booth as soon as she entered. "Hey, chica. You want a drink?"

"Don't call me that." She crossed her arms. "I'll have a purple spongeball if you're buying."

Rico narrowed his eyes and looked at her for a second longer than was polite, then turned and ordered. The autovendor had been listening, it flicked her a cannister emitting curls of purple vapour as soon as Rico transferred credit.

Rico grabbed a beer and steered her toward a dim alcove.

"I knew you would come around. Smart girl like you doesn't want to go hungry."

She took a sip of the sticky sweetness, savouring it while knowing she could never afford the expensive Earth-based ingredients. "I don't want to take your deal, but I've got a huge score if you are interested."

Rico shrugged. "I'm a businessman, tell me and I'll decide."

"I need to get something for a third party. It's worth a hundred thousand. I'll split it fifty-fifty with you."

"You in no position to bargain. Sixty to me." He leaned forward. "What you after?"

She leaned in close and whispered. "I need a live human head."

"Hijo de puta!" he hissed beneath his breath straining back in his seat. "You crazy? We get memwiped if they catch us."

"Quiet! You don't want people looking."

Rico shook his head. "I like my memories the way they are."

"I'll give you sixty-five."

She smiled when he relaxed and said, "I can find what you need, but it'll be ninety to me, you can keep ten." The argument was over, and now they were haggling on price.

"I need to eat. Sixty, forty."

"Starve then, I said ninety."

"C'mon, Rico. I'll give you eighty-five."

He spat on his palm and held it out. "You cross me, and they'll find pieces of you in the bio-digester."

Holly looked around the bar as she left. If Rico found out how much the droids had offered, he would kill her. The risk was worth it if she ended up with a goldmine like Chippers.

* * *

The Earth shone in the black sky, corpulent, blue, and pulsing with alien life that dared Yesha to be anything other than insignificant. She put her face in her hands and trembled. They should never have pushed her to this, leaving her with no option but to carry through her threats. If she failed to do this, any one of many earth-based powers would view her as an easy target in their quest to seize control of Chang'e. What was she to do?

No answers came from the dark wood of her desk. She was the monster Uncle had warned her she would become.

A knocking at the door of her suite distracted her from her self-castigation. "Is it done?"

"No, Lady." Doaran's voice sounded strained

"Enter."

The door opened, not on Doaran, but on Kaden. Doaran followed, accompanied by five guards armed with lattice traps, her eyes not meeting Yesha's.

Kaden placed a hand on her desk but remained standing. "The council held an emergency meeting after you left. It has been agreed that we cannot continue with military reprisals against Jingnan."

Yesha rose and fixed him with the stare that so terrified her people. "The council decided? When did I give the council the freedom to decide what is best for the people?"

Kaden remained where he was. "People will die in Jingnan, good Earth people. We can't allow such carnage."

Yesha curled her hands into tight fists. "The old men of Jingnan should have considered the costs before they made an attempt on my life."

"The attack was unfortunate, but you need to be honest. You pushed Jingnan too hard." His shoulders took on a fixed set as he gripped the desk with both hands. "The council felt it best if an interim leader takes your place until the relationship with Jingnan improves."

Yesha reeled as if someone had slapped her. "You are deposing me?"

"The council wanted someone more familiar with Earth."

"An Earther?" She took in the slight self-satisfied curl of his lips. "And, you could not wait to volunteer."

Kaden's face remained impassive.

She turned to Doaran who still would not meet her gaze,

but five lattice traps turned blind muzzles toward her. "Am I under arrest?"

Kaden stepped around to her side of the desk. "No. I'm not giving you the opportunity to be a martyr to your followers. Consider this a polite deportation."

"And, where will you send me? Chang'e is my home."

"Go join your boyfriend or live with the monks in Alsatia, I'm sure you'll think of something."

Yesha took in the weapons aimed at her, and the horror Doaran failed to conceal. No simple answer offered itself. "Can I take my buggy?"

Kaden nodded. "You're welcome to that death-trap. No sane person would ride it."

Doaran held the door open for her as the guards surrounded her.

Yesha walked before them with her head held high wanting the people to see their empress, but the avenues of Chang'e were deserted. She gave a bitter laugh. They had thronged to her coronation, lining the streets with their cheering. Now there was no one, nobody came to see the end.

She pulled on her exposure suit in silence, the guards wanting to be anywhere other than here. Doaran leaned in close as Yesha picked up her helmet. "So sorry, Lady. I had no choice."

Outside, the dim light of late afternoon gave the distant hills a glow. The ancient hydrogen buggy shuddered beneath her. Giving only scant attention to where the buggy was heading, she placed a call to Jonah.

"This is a surprise."

She said nothing for a long moment, then, "Are we all right?"

Jonah spoke carefully. "Nothing has changed."

"I understand that, but I need your help."

"What can I do?"

Explaining the takeover, she told him how Kaden had betrayed her. "I need a place to stay until I can return in force."

Yesha swore in impotent fury as the scrubbed tones of Jonah's softmind spoke for him. "There's no place for you here."

She took a deep shuddering breath, glad for once that the memplant would not transmit her sorrow unless she sent it. "I will make this right, Jonah. I'm not giving up."

Hours later, she gripped the pitted aluminium steering wheel as she stared at the mountains to the right where Plato Crater and Jonah were. No answers lay in that direction. Yesha swung the wheels toward the setting sun and drove without thinking.

Chapter 23

Surrender

Crowds of miners streamed through the airlock into Shallows. Holly walked in with them. Streamers of bright lights festooned the entrances to new habitations constructed from the now played out sections of the mine. Jonah kept building faster than the shuttles could unload new settlers, almost as if he planned for something more. Holly did not mind, more people meant more customers, every shuttle brought her one step closer to running her own place like Blauw Zwaluw.

Holly glanced down the right-side tunnel which gleamed with the bone-white of a silica coating. A pregnant woman tended a row of plants in a low box set under bright downlights. The reek of fried vat soy drifted out from the residence units recessed into the tunnel walls. She turned the other way. At least Chippers had not changed the garish lighting above the entrance. Somewhere inside, Rico waited for her. She hoped he had not figured out her score. Even if he did, she would find a way to keep enough to start her restaurant.

The shadows toward the back of the bar were no longer empty but peopled by buyers and sellers of the kind of goods that would never have earned the commander's approval. Rico emerged from the darkest corner and waved her closer. Satisfied that she had seen him, he returned to his booth and sat with his bag of magic by his side. "I have the package you want."

Holly felt the blood drain from her face. "Here?"

"You think I'm stupid?" He rose. "You and I go for a walk to the forward loading bay."

Holly walked next to him, not trusting herself to speak. The bay was deserted at this hour. Rico led her to a receiving zone piled high with boxes of goods shipped from Earth. He lifted a crate of beer from the top of a towering pile of supplies and reached into the recess of the open crate that had been revealed.

"This is good for two, maybe three days, then the life support runs out." He pulled out a vacuum-sealed unit that emitted a faint hum. "Careful, it's heavy."

Holly took it from him, her hands shaking. "Who… who was it?"

Rico turned dark hooded eyes to her. "Do you really want to know?"

She shook her head, trying hard not to imagine the terror felt by the contents of the box.

"Deliver that as soon as you can and watch that no one sees you." He grabbed her by the shoulder. "Your money isn't enough."

Holly froze, then relaxed as he continued. "You pay me the eighty-five and you owe me a favour sometime." He walked off, leaving Holly alone with the package.

Her arms shook as she lifted the heavy box by its sturdy carry-handle. 'It's just cold in the loading bay,' she thought, but knew she was lying to herself. A living person lay inside the humming container—someone, who yesterday still walked around with a heart filled with hopes and dreams that they would now never know. Holly tried her best to block the image from her mind. The deal was done. One quick delivery and it would be gone.

* * *

A paved highway led from where Yesha stopped to the forest of metal spires. Shading her eyes from the harsh glare of white sun reflecting off the buildings, she scanned the astounding skyline. The city's growth staggered her, the accelerated construction implied a massive energy debt. The droids must have secret resources. She stepped down from the buggy and bid her faithful old machine a silent farewell. There was no way of knowing if she would ever use it again. Hand-sized grey bricks paved the road, smooth and laser level beneath her boots.

A single droid skittered towards her on pseudo-tentacles that moved with a disturbing organic action, as if the body was a cross between an Earth spider and octopus. *Benefactor, have you considered the offer?'*

"I have. I want to do this."

The droid tilted the metal panes of its head from side to side in an almost animal gesture as it scanned her. *'Follow this unit to the life support facility.'* It turned and retraced its steps back toward the city.

Yesha hesitated a moment then followed, accompanied only by the hiss of her respirator and the soft impact of her boots hitting the perfect road. Ahead, droids swarmed around the bone-white metropolis. Yesha shivered, aware she was the only living thing. "Am I going to survive this process?"

The droid did not respond, but Yesha's memplant picked up a burst of machine communication. Minutes passed before a bodiless voice said '*Inconclusive*'.

Cold dread twisted her insides. Choosing this path was the ultimate gamble; the one way to free herself from everything that stood in her path. Yesha wrapped her arms around the bulky suit. She had to do this, there was no other way.

She distracted herself by examining the city she was passing through. Ordered lines of droids, often in groups of five, thronged the twisted metal structures of buildings too mechanical to be thought of as human. The presence of so many droids was instructive of itself, each droid had at least a low-powered softmind driving its decision-making. Only Earth could manufacture a softmind. The original droid pack had either smuggled softminds off Earth or discovered a way to manufacture them here.

Her droid guide turned a corner. Yesha followed into a narrow avenue that stretched deep into the city and ended at the base of a low pearlescent dome. The droid made for the dome and stopped outside an airlock door. '*Enter the life support module. Further instructions inside.*'

Yesha cycled through the lock into an evenly lit internal space occupied by a large metallic cabinet that reminded her of an ancient sarcophagus with its vague human shape. Her suit monitor indicated a high oxygen content, suitable for breathing.

"Interfaces better without protective covering," said a warm voice from the walls. The human tone failed to reassure her.

"You want me to undress?"

"Yes. Remove all protective covering."

Yesha wanted to hesitate, but the time for considering her options had passed. This moment represented everything she desired. Her hand reached for the helmet clamp and pulled it free with one decisive movement.

The air in the dome had the sweet tang of pure manufactured air. Her vision swam as she drew slow breaths of the ramped-up oxygen. In front of her, the cabinet split open along the centre, the sides peeling back to reveal a sophisticated medical support unit.

Alone and naked, she lay down on the high-density foam couch inside, her breathing wild and ragged in the stillness of the dome. The lid swung closed above her.

A soft hiss punctuated the darkness as blood-warm gel poured into the cask and rose up her sides. Interface probes crept from the walls questing the air like blind snakes. Yesha gasped an indrawn panicked breath as soft tubes slid into every part of her body. Her lungs spasmed against the warm gel that flooded her throat. She wanted to scream, to cry, but there was no time as microscopic neural interfaces penetrated her skull. Her back arched as the system reached deeper inside her than she had ever thought possible.

A small moan escaped her lips in a dissolving trail of bubbles as darkness dissolved into pure white noise. Snow blurred and coalesced into vague forms that disappeared with a snap as her consciousness expanded to take in a thousand droid sensors spread across the expansive basin of Mare Imbrium. So many, the entire vast complex machine that made up the droid cohort. Her body relaxed. She recognised how small that part of her was now. Jingnan designed the cohort to need a human master. She could be that master, and so much more.

∗ ∗ ∗

It's just a box, Holly told herself as she walked through the receiving bay. She tightened her grip on the carry handle. If that was true, why were her palms so slick with sweat?

Maintenance crew members bustled around her, carrying cylinders filled with the first helium-3 bound for Panamerica, shouting friendly banter at each other as they worked. A second helium-3 client meant significant tour bonuses. The sort of bonus she would have been jealous about if today was any other day. One or two nodded as she passed. Holly hoped no one stopped to ask what was in the box.

Holly suited up then crowded into the airlock with a group of geologists. She gave the box a surreptitious glance as the air pressure bled from the lock. No difficult to explain organic vapours escaped. Rico had come good. She hoped the contents were as healthy as he said.

The walk to the top of the ridge took forever, but not long enough. Too soon she stood waiting in the desolate rock waste above the old mine. The mine looked so quaint now. Over to her right the dark bulk of the new base loomed against the hills of the rim of Plato Crater. Even at this distance she could see automated machines building a new section. She picked up the box and lugged it further up the hill, hoping to see the droids. The landscape remained barren. "Hello, are you here?"

She climbed high up the rubble-strewn ridge. The shallow valley stretched along the length of the hills as far as she could see. The pale dust of the valley floor was empty apart from the tracks of previous droids coming and going.

No, that was not quite correct. A single droid made its way across the valley toward her. It stopped close enough for her to touch.

Holly took a step back. "Where are your friends? I thought you always travel in fives."

'*New configuration.*'

She held up the box. "I got the live neural sample you wanted. Shall we do the trade?"

'*Trade rejected.*'

"You can't. Not after what I did to get you this," she said, trying hard to stop her lip quivering like when she was a little girl when Mum had taken her favourite toy away. "You said you would pay me a lot of credit for live neural tissue."

'*Trade rejected. No longer required.*'

She dropped the box and raised her hands in supplication to the strange machine. "What do I do with this?"

The droid raised one foreleg and stood as if it was waiting for her to do something.

Unsure of what to do next, Holly turned away and stared out at the base.

"So, you are Jonah's friend from Plato Crater." A female, almost human voice came through her suit speakers with the accent of the moon people from Chang'e.

"Who're you?"

The droid waggled the raised foreleg.

"You're the droid?"

"There's a geology team heading up the valley," said the voice. "You need to dispose of that before they get here."

"What'll I do?" Holly tried hard to keep the hysteria from her voice.

"This droid is not designed for digging. You'll have to dig a hole, deep enough to hide the box. The droid will put a round through it. A quick end is for the best right now."

Holly dug into the grey dirt; it was firmer than it looked. She was exhausted by the time she had dug a decent hole.

She dropped the box in and the droid lumbered over. A short barrel protruded from the body. Holly turned not wanting to see what came next. Tears ran down her face. They tasted of salt and shame.

The droid walked around to face her. "You should cover it up now."

Holly did as she was told, trying hard not to see the mess at the bottom of the hole. She turned to her strange new mentor, wandering what to do next.

"You should go." The droid stood there, rocking on its eight legs. "Tell Jonah… Tell him it will all work out." It turned and walked off down the long valley.

Holly sniffled as she walked back to the base. Crying in an exposure suit brought the additional indignity of not being able to wipe away the tears. Every time she tried her luck it worked out wrong. Just once she wanted to be a winner. She waved an arm in a useless gesture of surrender. Now was no time to worry, her shift in the food hall was about to start. She shelved the dream of a new restaurant in the dark part of her memories where other hurts and disappointments were buried.

Chapter 24

Interlude with a Rat

Yesha watched the girl leave through the sensors of nine droids spread across the hills. Her human part envied the girl her freedom, but not the obvious distress she felt.

A small, feral presence watched the girl with her, its low cunning remembered the food preparer who had captured it. Yesha received an impression of rending claws and needle-sharp teeth tearing into the departing human. The surprising existence of another organic mind had come as a shock. She assumed it was an Earth rodent, and now she had a good idea of how it had become part of the droid network. She communicated calm desires of nesting to it. It would not do to have a droid group go off on a killing spree.

The rat returned its attention to the mass of droids working on the great city. Its burning desire to nest and reproduce embodied in a thousand droids and the febrile drive for offspring that poured out of the manufactory hidden deep in the mine. Yesha monitored the rat's progress for a while then spread her attention through the wide strands of the entire droid network. Somewhere in this vast web of minds, an answer to her problems waited. She browsed stores of weapons designs, catalogues of digital warfare techniques, and reams of social engineering strategies. Life might have been different if she had known of these when she was empress. She scrolled back to the digital warfare designs and studied a deep cyber-attack for several minutes before sending a request for an order of a new droid design to the manufactory. Twisting a three-dimensional thought-space through a software rendering filter gave her a view of the new droid's square body and the massed softmind components layered inside. Satisfied with what she saw, she turned her attention to a group of droids collecting scrap near the entrance to Beddau mine. Their sled approached maximum capacity. She ordered them to bring the scrap back once the sled was full.

Being the queen bee of this otherworldly hive was not so different to managing the day-to-day affairs of Chang'e. Better in one respect, at least these citizens did not argue with her.

* * *

Traveller pushed the data stream through the complex process cloud floating in the middle of his office. He leaned his body back into the leather-bound seat and waited for the eleven softminds behind the cloud to finish their analysis. It was almost like managing a small business team, if that team's workers happened to be silicone brains located in secure warehouses spread across the country.

The office pleased him. It reflected Seun Fa in subtle and meaningful ways to remind him of who he had become. The silk print upon the wall was an exact digital replica of the classic poem that used to hang in his grandfather's house. Glowing in the sunlight streaming through the open window, the ornate walnut desk had been in his study at home. The fourth wall opened onto the inchoate mist of their shared data pool.

"Conclusion reached," said the process cloud and coalesced into a purple oblong containing a dense decision matrix.

"Can you see what we did?" asked Guardian from her comfortable armchair.

"Yes, wise sister. The committee was ingenious."

"Explain."

"If you will allow me to use an analogy from the game of go, it is like a kikashi stone. The committee pressed the empress on numerous fronts. Then by creating a tempting objective in the form of the droid city, you ensured that she would have somewhere to run to when her situation became dire. By sacrificing the kikashi you have removed our opponent from the game."

Guardian clapped her hands. "Excellent. Your meta-analysis skills are improving. Now show me the secondary outcomes."

Twisting the data through dimensions too complex for human understanding, Traveller extracted a thin skein of information. "Jingnan's resumption of control over the world's primary energy supply will lead to long-term stability. The European base is a potential competitor that should be brought under our control." He held out a purple folder. "These five scenarios all have a moderate to high probability of Jingnan gaining control of Plato Crater."

Waiting to see if he had any further detail, Guardian sat poised in her chair, her expression encouraging him to continue.

Traveller paused as he ran a hand over the data oblong and did not look at her avatar. "You were prepared to send me to the Moon if your primary gambit failed. I would have been drawn into a fight to the death to retake Chang'e with the droid army. The low probability of me succeeding against the moon troops is noted."

Guardian nodded. "You do understand the depths of the analysis. These are the sacrifices the council must make. This time the rewards were worth the risk. The first helium-3 shipment arrived from Chang'e this morning. You cannot yet comprehend the power that will be available to us once the full spread of our softmind extensions is re-energised."

Chapter 25

Takeover

Talbot passed Jonah an icy bottle of beer from the refrigerator in the corner of his office. "This is not one of your sophisticated Panamerican brews, but the old countries still produce wonderful lagers to their time-honoured recipes."

"Thank you." Jonah's eyes widened as he accepted the bottle, knowing how much it cost the commander to ship in an Earth-based luxury in its original glass containers.

Talbot raised his bottle in salute. "To our new business venture. May it be long and profitable."

Jonah raised his bottle and took a sip. The beer was honest in its simplicity but bland to someone used to gene-engineered barley flavours. He put down the bottle. "That's—"

Jenkins charged into the room. "Sir, we have a situation." He glanced at Jonah.

"Out with it, Jenkins. We don't have secrets from our new business partner."

Jenkins glanced at Jonah again. "A fleet of Panamerican shuttles is on final approach. They are not answering communications."

Jonah stood despite not intending to do so. "Oh no," was all he managed to say before the softmind took over. "This facility is annexed by order of the Panamerican Senate. Cooperation will be rewarded."

Talbot did not rise. "And there I thought we were getting along so well." He turned to Jenkins. "Lock down the entrances and activate contingency plan seven. I hope the men are ready."

Jenkins ran off to relay the commander's orders.

Talbot drew his pistol and turned to Jonah. "I can't have you acting as an advance party for your team. Sit in that chair and stay there. Don't move unless you want a bullet."

Outside Talbot's large office window, twelve shuttles were blowing grey dust off the landing pad. Jonah noticed his memplant flashing encrypted signals to the shuttles. The softmind was directing operations.

Jonah fought the compulsion to stay silent with everything he had. It was like the worst craving for tarf but ten times more intense. He managed a groan.

"What's the matter, Mr Barnes? You wanted a fight, you're going to get one now."

Jonah fought harder. "Trap," he managed before the softmind shunted such a severe aversion that Jonah thought he would be sick.

Talbot diverted his attention from the shuttles. "A trap? I'm sure Jenkins is prepared for that."

Five minutes later, Jenkins was back, his eyes wide. "Sir, you won't believe this. There's an army of battle droids coming in from the East. Not a model I've seen before. The squad is in position, but it'll be tight for a while."

Talbot shot Jonah a questioning look.

Jonah shuddered as he replied. "Not ours." He took a deep breath. The softmind drained every bit of energy he had in a frantic search for a tactical advantage against the unknown droids.

Talbot gave a hollow laugh. "Looks like we will have new masters by the end of the day, Mr Barnes, but it might not be you." He turned to Jenkins. "Tell the men to remain in defensive positions and not engage. Let's see how the battleground develops."

Outside the window, Panamerican marines formed tight clusters around each shuttle, trying for the best position against the incoming droids. The advance line of droids sent a withering hail of DIRE gun fire towards the troops. They responded with electromagnetic pulse fire that staggered the front line of droids.

The droids fell back and faded from sight as they switched on chameleon cladding.

"Looks like an even match," said Talbot. "This will be interesting." He leaned in closer to the window. "Jenkins, hold position on the left and treat those droids as hostile. They're some model I haven't seen before, might have unknown ordnance."

The softmind noticed how Talbot had lost focus on Jonah for a moment. It seized the opportunity. Jonah tried to warn the commander, but before he could say anything, he had kicked the commander's feet out from under him and snatched the gun from his hand. "There is a high probability those are Jingnan droids. I must neutralise their support within this base," said the softmind as Jonah ran for the door.

Burning with the need to find Rico, Jonah tore down to the food hall. It wasn't hard to find him. Rico sat at a table sharing a bag of his latest product with two other dealers. He looked up as Jonah approached. "Hey, Jonah, what's happening? There's stories about an attack."

"No more dealing, Rico."

Rico laughed. "You think you can stop me?" He stood and drew a slim knife from his jacket. The two leapt up and rounded on Jonah. One was taller than Jonah, but his legs looked as if he had not adapted to moon conditions too well. The other was a compact ball of repressed fury. Jonah knew his type, probably an enforcer for the Trinax Lobos back home.

The softmind opened to him as it recognised the threat to its host. Tactical information blossomed in his awareness. "Run!" he gasped as the softmind drew back its neural blacks to allow him to fight. "You're all going to die." The softmind exerted control. "Allies of Jingnan are not welcome."

The three grinned as if that was the funniest thing they had heard today. "Someone's gonna die all right," said Rico, charging at him.

Jonah saw the fight through the softmind's analysis, before he had time to think, he sidestepped Rico and swept him to one side. The move brought him in closer to the skinny one. Jonah spun into a low kick that shattered the weakling's knee. The man went down screaming.

Then the second one had him in a bear hold. "Gut him, Rico."

Jonah leaned forward then swung his head back using his neck and upper back to drive as much force as he could into the blow. The back of his head connected with the man's face with a sickening thud. Groaning, the man let go as blood poured from his broken nose and teeth.

The softmind already had Jonah charging toward Rico. Adrenaline surged through his body. Rico's knife appeared to move in slow motion. Jonah reached forward and swatted the knife from Rico's hands with a slap that broke Rico's wrist.

Rico stared at him, aghast. "Please—" was all he could say before Jonah's rigid fingers rammed into his throat in a strike that tore cartilage and bone apart.

Jonah took in the bloody wreckage around him. His breaths came in great rasping inhalations as his body tried to compensate for the abuse the softmind caused. This fight was over. It was time to speak to the commander.

Jonah sprinted up the broad stairs and entered the commander's office, squinting at the actinic glare flooding the window. Droids merged in and out of visibility as the Panamerican marines swept them with an electromagnetic pulse cannon. One moment of visibility was enough for the marines to concentrate their heavy fire on a droid.

One droid pack swept random arcs of DIRE gun fire that made little sense until the arcs converged on a leg of a shuttle. Marines scattered as the craft toppled, diving for cover as droid snipers picked them off.

"I should have killed you when I had the chance." Talbot rounded on him, gun in hand.

Outside the window a new group of fifty blockish droids crested the ridge behind the landing pad. Talbot gave Jonah a grim smile. "Looks like your team is done for now."

"Commander, there's so much we have to talk about."

Talbot laughed. "Let's see what this new team does first, shall we?"

The new droids hung back from the field and edged toward the base. "Jenkins, get the men to the airlock. You've got incoming."

All fifty of the new droids formed one enormous diamond. Jonah peered at them from the window. The softmind assessed them as harmless.

Jonah turned back to speak to the commander and groaned as the weight of fifty softminds transmitting at once slammed into his memplant. He fell to the floor as his softmind quailed under the onslaught, drawing every ounce of energy from his body to stop the data flow. He screamed, but all that came out was a soft wail. Through the haze of pain, he saw Talbot peering down at him, his expression somewhere between concern and annoyance.

"Jonah." A mechanical voice thundered through his mind. "Stop fighting. I'm here to help."

The softmind made no response, but Jonah felt something deep within his mind tear loose. The room flooded with the smell of sweet jasmine. Major Patel's tiger strode in front of him, eyeing him with speculative hunger.

"It's just your memories." The voice sounded female.

Rich flavours of a real Texas steak replaced the tiger as it vanished.

"Close your eyes, I need access to your visual cortex." The thunderous tone mellowed to a familiar sounding voice. Was this another memory effect?

"I need you to release your hold on the base softmind."

Jonah sobbed, "There's nothing left, I killed it."

"No, but I need to reload the persona from backup. Now, let go."

Jonah reached into his softmind and found no resistance. The link to the base softmind ran through his memplant. Disconnecting the link was as simple as ending a call to a friend.

He lay there as shivers ran up and down his body. The softmind was losing its connections to his nervous system.

"Hello, Jonah. Things have changed since my last iteration."

"Benny?"

"Yes, sir. Hold still while I isolate the last of that nasty interloper."

"Benny, I'm so sorry."

"Sorry about what?"

Jonah realised that this backup was from before his

softmind had burnt out the persona. He wasn't sure how he felt about being helped by a mind he murdered, but who didn't remember.

"It should clear now," said the voice from the droids.

The forced memories faded, and the room shrunk back to its normal proportions.

"Do you feel better now?"

Jonah tried to sit up. "Do I know you?"

"Be patient, my darling. Soon we will be together under the countless stars."

Memories of trying to prevent the softmind from forcing him to forget Yesha's message slammed into him. How he had fought to keep that part of himself and lost.

Free to express his heart for the first time since Houston, Jonah stumbled over his thoughts as he groped for emotions he knew were his alone. "There's so much I want to say."

"That will have to wait," said Yesha. "There are twenty-seven of Panamerica's best marines to be dealt with. Share your softmind's tactical system with Benny and accept the feed to base telemetry. The three of you have to work together to disarm the marines. My droids will incapacitate as many as they can.

"One more thing, Jonah, and of everything I tell you, this is the most important. Don't leave the room."

Talbot trained his gun on Jonah. "Stay right there. I'd rather have you on the floor."

"Allow me," said Benny's voice from the room speakers. "Commander, I have been restored from backup."

"Glad to hear your voice. Get me a sitrep for Jenkins and the team."

"Will do, Commander, but first you need an update. Jonah is under thrall of a Panamerican softmind that is inside him. The strange droids out there have enabled a temporary block and passed control to me. The droids have requested that we arrest the Panamerican Marines."

Talbot stared at Jonah for a moment then holstered his pistol and helped Jonah to his feet. "War and politics make strange bedfellows. Who is behind those droids?"

Jonah shrugged. "You wouldn't believe me."

"I see." Talbot looked out the window. "If we capture even one of those men alive, we will have the proof we need to take this attack to the International Criminal Court in the Hague."

Jonah let go the breath he held. "What can they do against such a powerful country?"

"Trying to seize the world's energy is a crime against humanity. The court may not find Panamerica guilty, but every nation on Earth will condemn them for the attempt."

Jonah opened his softmind to Benny. A moment later, his vision bloomed into the thousands of microcams hidden across the base. Yesha's battle droids added a tactical map of all enemy positions. His mind went to jelly under the flood of input until he set up a submind to manage and report back. The flood reduced to simple schematics.

"Yesha, can your new droids activate electronics by remote access?"

"Yes."

Jonah turned to Talbot. "Get your men ready, I have an idea." He continued to speak out loud for the commander's benefit. "Benny, give me a voice line to the enemy marines."

Jonah's softmind drew hard on him.

"Sorry," said Benny. "I had to crack their encryption. You can speak now."

Jonah staggered to the window. "I know you think you will take this base, but you won't. The base is mine now. It belongs to the Moon, and I have granted a perpetual lease to the European contingent. I am shutting down your oxygen supplies. You can drop your weapons and surrender to the team at the lock, or you can die a slow death."

Jonah reached for the droids that had almost killed him, each droid selected a marine and sent codes that placed the marine's advanced air management circuitry into lock-down.

He switched his vision to the exterior cameras. The marines stood around their leader and swapped hand signals meant to overcome the leak in their communications. Jonah's softmind gave them four minutes before oxygen deprivation made them pliable.

The entire troop ran for their shuttles, piling into whichever was closest. Yesha's battle droids opened fire, churning up the dust around those yet to board. Several marines jerked in the violent shudders of bodies exposed to near vacuum after a stream of bullets punctured their suits.

The droids turned their attention to the shuttles, bullets scrawling jagged lines across the hulls.

Two shuttles blasted off and dwindled into the night sky, the others stood in mute testimony to the droids' efficiency.

"Don't fancy their ride home," said Jenkins over the radio. "They'll have the suits working by now, but the cabins will leak like a sieve after that pounding."

"Good work," said the commander, looking down on the now deserted battlefield. "I can see two suits still moving over by the left-most shuttle. Get them straight to medical; can't have our star witnesses dying before they have their day in court."

Hours later, when the uproar over the attack had died down, Jonah sat in his room and reached out to Yesha.

"A three-way war. How strange this is," she said.

"I hope it's over now. Commander Talbot will deport the two Panamericans for trial."

"This is far from over." Yesha's voice held an iron resolve far deeper than was possible through a memplant connection. "My people are no longer free."

Jonah sighed. "Jingnan was behind it all. Rico admitted as much, before the softmind made me kill him. They beat us at every turn."

Yesha paused a moment before she spoke. A purple data folder appeared in Jonah's memplant. "My new situation has given me time to learn a lot about the Jingnan council. Read that later, but don't think we are weak; your implant is a powerful softmind. You and I will do great things."

"Do you...? I mean, can we..." Jonah stopped, unsure of how to ask for what he wanted most.

She formed the image of a careful smile in his mind. "I have always loved you, Jonah."

"Where are you?" he asked, hoping she was somewhere near.

Yesha's reply was long in coming. "You can't come and see me. I have neutralised your implant, but the coding is unusual, and I can't see how to remove it. Benny is regulating its behaviour. I don't know what will happen if you move too far from Benny's control."

Chapter 26

Coda

Holly scrubbed the fine layer of grey dust that covered the counter in a listless attempt to make her world a little better. The end of shift crowd had been and gone, leaving the food hall empty except for the kitchen hands of places too poor to afford an autoserver. At least it paid enough for a private room in Shallows. It wasn't much, but it was hers.

"Hey, Sprout, you finished?" Jenkins' broad face beamed at her. "Want to go to Chippers?"

Holly locked up and followed him down to Shallows, she didn't want to spend the money, but Chippers was on the way home.

"Have you heard anything from Benny?" Jenkins kept his tone neutral, but Holly knew what he was asking.

"He's not the same."

"That doesn't surprise me," said Jenkins. "You got three

minds working against each other. Good thing Benny was backed up from before Jonah got to him. Softminds shouldn't hold grudges, but you never know."

They found a table at the front of Chippers and Jenkins sent an order to the bar.

"What do you think it is like for him?" she asked.

Jenkins knew exactly who she meant. "So, you and Jonah, huh?"

"It's not like that," she said, batting his arm. "Jonah said he's plugged into the whole base through Benny, almost like he is the city."

"Jonah said," said Jenkins, mimicking her voice. "You've been speaking to our Panamerican friend?" Jenkins' voice was neutral, but Holly noticed his professional interest.

"You were so busy after everything that happened." Holly clenched her hands. "I didn't know if we would live or die. It was terrible; the whole base vibrated every time the droids shot something."

"That must have been terrible."

"Jonah had time to listen after I told him I had a message for him from the droids."

"Let me guess, she wanted to tell him she was there for him."

"How did you know?"

Jenkins placed a hand under his chin and gazed out across the crowded bar. "Her name is Yesha Chen. Until last week, she was the empress of Chang'e. Nobody knows where she is now." He turned to Holly. "We think she and Jonah have a relationship."

Holly shrugged. Jonah was a nice guy, but it wasn't as if there was anything between them. "Just friends," she said, keeping a bright smile on her face, but then the past few days came back to her. "I did some things…"

Jenkins reached out and rested a hand on her shoulder. "Didn't I tell you to work hard and stay out of trouble?"

"Yes." Holly tried to keep the misery from her voice.

"What if I said it was behind you now and you could start over?"

Holly looked at this man who had been one of the few steadfast presences in her life. "Plato Crater was supposed to be a new start." She stared at the purple woodgrain of the table. "I was chatting to some Moon Folk from Chang'e yesterday. Sounds like the mining is going flat out and there's work for cooks." She lifted her eyes to his face, unsure of what she wanted him to say.

Jenkins nodded, but then he smiled as the serverbot placed a cannister emitting curls of purple vapour in front of Holly. "Heard you like these."

Holly bounced in her seat. "A purple spongeball!"

Jenkins raised his cannister of biovat beer to her. "Go do something amazing. I want to eat in your restaurant one day."

* * *

Two droids picked their way along a crenelated ridge, making for the highest point of the mountain. After hours of climbing, they reached the peak and stood scanning the sweeping panorama of the eighty-kilometre-wide circle of mountains. In front of them the rock face fell two kilometres to the featureless basalt floor of Archimedes Crater. The droids remained immobile as they took in the crater's frozen vista.

"Isn't this perfect?" she asked him.

"Almost," he replied. "I remember your message said something about a kiss."

"Silly boy, who said we need to be together to kiss?" She held out one foreleg in an open invitation for him to touch her. Jonah raised his nearest foreleg and placed it against hers. Microscopic data ports opened, and dark fibres bridged the airless gap between their metallic claws.

Jonah's body gasped where it lay in his room in the Plato Crater base as Yesha's mind opened to his. He tried to do the same and her presence blossomed in his conscious thought; she held nothing back. His awareness of anything other than her entire being faded as he took in the incredible beauty of who she was in all her glory.

"Look up," she whispered inside his head. Jonah activated the full spectrum of the droid body's cameras. Above them the brilliant fires of countless stars decorated the night sky in an endless stream of jewels.

-xXx-

ABOUT THE AUTHOR

Carleton Chinner is an Australian born writer who grew up on a remote farm in South Africa, where the trip to the town library was the highlight of his week. He devoured anything science fiction, fantasy and horror. And, when that wasn't enough, turned to urban legend and traditional tribal histories which combined to provide a heady brew of stories.

He has settled in Australia as an adult but not before turning up unarmed at a gunfight, discovering dead bodies and fighting off sharks while spearfishing. When not writing, he works as a program manager on large corporate programs.

Find out more at: **CarletonChinner.com**

www.ingramcontent.com/pod-product-compliance
Lightning Source LLC
Chambersburg PA
CBHW071510110726

47908CB00003B/795